the deceit

Books by Sara Foster

the deceit
SARA FOSTER

BLACK STONE
PUBLISHING

The characters and events in this book are fictitious.
Any similarity to real persons, living or dead, is coincidental
and not intended by the author.

Printed in the United States of America

First edition: 2023
ISBN 979-8-200-89563-2
Fiction / Thrillers / Domestic

Version 1

CIP data for this book is available
from the Library of Congress

Blackstone Publishing
31 Mistletoe Rd.
Ashland, OR 97520

www.BlackstonePublishing.com

In memory of Pippa
and for Avalon and Annwyn
with all my love

chapter one

LENNY

Lenny wakes to the sound of glass breaking. It's barely daylight and he sits bolt upright, his first thought that the twins are up and messing around. Or Claire has dropped something in her rush to leave. But then there's another crash, and he realizes it's coming from outside.

Aware of the cold, empty space beside him, he swings his legs out of bed, bare feet resting on the cold tiles. He allows himself a moment to let his body adjust, then strides across to the window, opening the blind a fraction, hoping he's being discreet enough that whoever is out there won't notice.

On the opposite side of the road, a man and a woman crouch, gathering pieces of glass from the remains of two broken bottles. Liquid oozes across the bitumen. The man straightens and says something to the woman's back, but she appears to ignore him. In response, the man throws up his hands, returning to the open rear doors of a large white van and pulling out two dining chairs, which he then inexplicably abandons on the tarmac while he disappears inside the house.

If these are the new neighbors, this doesn't bode well, Lenny thinks to himself, his fleeting thoughts of new friends, drinks, and barbecues shattering in front of him. From his vantage point, he can make out the woman's thick cropped black hair, and the oversized gray sweater she wears over long black leggings. While she continues picking up glass, the man reappears and jumps back inside the van, ignoring the chairs and collecting another cardboard box. He's solid muscle, with an upright posture and everything flexed, his broad shoulders bulging as he carts the box up to the front door and inside. Lenny becomes momentarily aware of his own slender arms and torso, and he's about to turn away when the man marches back into view, his face a grimace as he snaps something at the woman. She scowls up at him and seems to slow the pace of her glass collection in retaliation. The man stands observing her for a moment, arms folded, then storms away toward the house. Alone again, the woman seems to suddenly sense Lenny's gaze and glances up toward him. And although the blinds are open the merest crack, Lenny jumps back as though stung.

Embarrassed about snooping, he leaves them to it, but he can't help his disappointment. He'd had high hopes in the weeks the redbrick house had stood empty, since elderly Lottie Jenkins had died in her bed. Lottie had set out her stall as the street's local busybody, and until she'd gone Lenny hadn't realized how self-conscious he'd become while wrangling the twins in and out of the car, or delivering the bins to the curb while still in his pajamas. He'd been thankful that Lottie only moved slowly, so he could usually get back inside by the time she reached her door, because if she collared him, he'd had to listen to various tales of woe about her declining physical health or discuss the shocking behavior of the always-arguing Allett family two doors down. Or, if Lottie was in a particularly snippy mood, she would admonish him for being a house-husband and for Claire's lack of quality time around the children.

Lenny grabs a T-shirt, pulls it on, and heads to the kitchen, wincing as his foot is stabbed by an errant piece of Lego. Claire's empty cup sits in the sink, and he touches the ceramic to find it cold. *Who the hell wants to train at this time?* he wonders, glancing out as the first glow of daylight drifts across their backyard. He turns on the coffee machine, which responds with a metallic groan that makes him wince. As always, he prays it won't disturb the kids. He likes his first coffee in peace—in fact, the day always seems to go better when he manages it.

The house remains quiet, and Lenny makes his drink quickly, efficient and practiced at the ritual. He takes the steaming mug with him and goes to sit on the back step, watching as the garden wakes up. There are always a couple of willy wagtails around first thing, singing *djiti djiti* to him as they wiggle their tiny tail feathers. Today they chase each other across the grass and across the detritus of discarded plastic play equipment, and Lenny smiles as he watches them.

Behind him, the vivarium in the corner buzzes to life as the timers click on, illuminating a small bearded dragon on a branch. "Morning, Bob," Lenny says, as the creature cocks his head, one small black eye trained on Lenny. "Get warmed up, and then I'll get you some crickets."

His phone buzzes from the countertop, interrupting the peace of the morning. He tries to drink his coffee before checking it, but just knowing the message is there is unbearable, an unscratched itch, and despite his best intentions, he finds himself going to grab the phone, bringing it back to the step. This time it's a message from the bank, asking him to check his emails, which sounds ominous. *Great.* And there's one from Claire too, reminding him about the rental inspection.

He looks around at the place. *Damn.* The agent will be at him again to fix the hole in the wall that Jake made with a tennis racket after losing his temper. Lenny doesn't want to tell them that he's shit at DIY and they can't afford to pay a contractor for the repair yet. That nothing has changed in the last few months.

He texts Claire back, telling her the house inspection is under control. Thinks of adding a line about the new neighbors but doesn't. She'll be busy with clients, and anyway, he's done sending chatty messages and only receiving curt replies.

He still can't believe they've reached this point. Strangers living in the same house. Sharing a bed. Going through the motions of normality for the sake of the kids. And he won't blame the kids for the implosion of their marriage, even though he knows in his heart that they were one of the main reasons things changed.

When they'd first moved to this quiet spot of Perth suburbia, ten years ago, Claire would sit here on the back step with him in the morning, looking out at the garden, both of them content just to be together and watch the world. She'd seemed happy back then, and he'd loved her so much. But he thought he knew her wholeheartedly too, and now he isn't so sure.

He hesitates, then flicks through his messages to the

number he doesn't recognize and scans the texts he's been getting for the last couple of weeks, which he's yet to share with anyone.

> Your wife is a liar.

> Has your wife told you the truth yet?

> Do you know who Claire really is?

Since the messages started coming, he's had one most days, always early in the morning. After the first few, he'd replied, asking, "*Who is this?*" but they never responded. He'd called the number but it just rang out. In the beginning, he'd hoped it was a random troll: he'd had enough emails and phone calls to know there were plenty of phishing schemes out there that baited people with threats and suggestions as a path to blackmail or fraud. But now there are twelve in total, and the phone is a grenade sitting in his hand, waiting for him to set off the explosion.

He knows he should show the messages to Claire, but the thought is terrifying. Is he ready to detonate the kids' lives? His life? Because he's certain there are things Claire hasn't told him. There have been too many questions she can't or won't answer; or the occasional stray phrase that doesn't match the majority of the stories she's shared about her childhood. Even these tales were few and far between, because she'd said early on that her background was painful, and she didn't want to talk about it.

He'd tried to be understanding and hadn't pressed it—something he regrets—because he'd thought she would explain eventually. But he's never found a way to reach her. And now they're in trouble, with two young kids who love and depend on them both.

He walks through the house to check on each sleeping child in turn. Emily's arms are wrapped around Geoffrey the giraffe; while Jake lies splayed like a starfish, lost in his dreams. At the sight of their innocent little faces, he feels a painful tug in his chest.

He heads toward the bathroom to begin getting dressed and ready for the day but stops short at the sight of his exhausted face in the mirror. Why, he asks his reflection, would an anonymous stranger want to goad him into lighting this fuse and blowing up his family, even if their life together has been built on lies? He closes his eyes, shutting out the world so he can steady himself. However much he wants to know the truth, he's not sure he's brave enough to demand it. And once he does, he's afraid there'll be no going back.

chapter two

CLAIRE

Claire watches in resignation as Elizabeth struggles on the treadmill. The woman's face is beetroot red, her skin sheened with sweat. She wears bright yoga pants and a neon pink vest top, and the fat around her belly jiggles up and down as her feet slap against the rubber surface.

"One more minute," Claire calls, and Elizabeth nods furiously, unable to speak, eyeballs bursting from their sockets with this final effort.

Behind Elizabeth, through the window, the sky is a tepid gray. There's supposed to be scattered showers all week, but, as always, Claire hopes the forecast is wrong. Late autumn downpours cause havoc with her outdoor classes.

The treadmill stops whirling and Elizabeth staggers from it, grabbing a towel and bending over, hands on her knees, trying to catch her breath.

"You did good," Claire says reassuringly, although she'd

hoped they would have been upping these speeds a lot more by now. Elizabeth is committed to the training, but the diet is a challenge for someone who loves to lunch and drink wine with her friends. Her husband owns the biggest real estate agency in Perth, and she doesn't need to work to enjoy her lavish lifestyle. This home gym is bigger than most of the studios Claire works in; you could squeeze at least thirty people and their yoga mats in here.

As Elizabeth recovers, she looks Claire up and down. "I'm sure you get skinnier by the week."

Claire laughs. "You say that every time. If it were true, I'd be all bone by now."

"Perhaps I'm just getting fatter every week." Elizabeth looks at herself disparagingly in the full-length floor-to-ceiling mirror that runs down one side of the gym. "How can I be getting fatter when I pay you all this money?"

Claire sighs inwardly. Elizabeth likes to throw these frustrated barbed comments at her, post-workout, while the adrenaline is still firing. She'd rather blame Claire for the lack of results than commit to working harder on the diet.

"I don't think you're getting fatter. But if you're not getting the results you want, are you sure you're committed to every part of the training? We talked through the three pillars: it's exercise, diet, and sleep." They both know it's the diet, but Claire wants to be kind.

"You've forgotten genetics," Elizabeth adds snippily. "My mum's been plus size since I was born—what hope have I got, really? I bet your mum's as thin as a rake."

Claire tenses, as she always does when the conversation ventures near family. Ever since she moved to Western

Australia, only one person within five thousand kilometers of her has known any of her history beyond the last decade, and she hasn't seen Devon in over nine years. Claire has memorized a doctored version of her childhood, reconstructed to appease any curious parties while making sure she doesn't easily get caught in the lies. But she doesn't want to get into any of this with Elizabeth. "Are you sure you're sleeping enough?" she tries instead.

Elizabeth turns away. "I've had a few broken nights, I suppose," she mumbles.

Claire would like to add that the alcohol won't help the sleep either, but she can see Elizabeth bristling, and chooses not to antagonize her. It would be nice to keep this gig, since it's one of the better-paid ones. "Look, weigh in on Monday, like usual, and then why don't we do a full assessment next week?"

Elizabeth nods. "Okay, but let's wait until the week after. It's the Telethon Gala on Sunday."

Claire accepts the excuse and delay, mentally adding it to the pile that has arisen during the last three months of training. She grabs her bag, hoping to get out quickly, but before she can make a move, the gym door opens.

Jarrod stands there in suit and tie, appraising them both. He's the opposite of his wife, all sinew and muscle. Elizabeth has told Claire that he spends most evenings here in the gym, working off the frustrations of the day. He's a real estate entrepreneur, now CEO of Shipman & Fine, a company that oversees a large proportion of the city's property sales and rentals, including Claire and Lenny's house. She's only come across Jarrod fleetingly so far: once passing in the hallway, and once getting in and out of their cars, but even his smile makes Claire uncomfortable. If he catches her alone, the accompanying flicker of his eyes across her is always suggestive. And if she's with Elizabeth, Jarrod's disdain for his wife is obvious.

"I'm leaving," he says to Elizabeth, before he flashes a grin at Claire and asks, "How did her workout go?"

"Good," Claire says quickly. "Elizabeth always puts in max effort."

"I should hope so, for what she's paying you," he says. "It'll be great when it starts showing."

Claire's stance shifts and straightens. She won't let him see her unease around him, instinctively understanding how much he would enjoy it. "You know, what might help is if she had some encouragement," she suggests. "Some couples like to work out together and motivate each other."

Jarrod laughs openly. "Keep going, Elizabeth," he calls across the room, smirking, his gaze still fixed on Claire, before he closes the door.

The women stare after him for a moment, before Elizabeth breaks the silence. "He's such a wanker," she says, grabbing a small towel and rubbing it across her neck. "I'm sorry."

Claire shrugs. "I've met worse."

In the silence that follows, she grows nervous under Elizabeth's curious gaze. Perhaps Elizabeth is wondering about Claire's husband, which almost makes her laugh out loud, because Lenny could not be more different from posturing Jarrod and all the other alpha males she's had the misfortune to come across. All Lenny wants to do is love her, she thinks with a pang. How had that become so unbearable?

Elizabeth interrupts Claire's thoughts, saying quietly, "I don't just stay for the money. I mean, of course, it's important, and I love this house. But the kids are almost grown and can't wait to get out of here. I could leave too, and I'm sure I'd get a nice settlement through a lawyer. But . . ." she pauses, as though figuring out exactly what to say, "Jarrod isn't someone you want as your enemy. He likes being in charge . . . you should see him when he gets outsmarted by someone. He's too used to power and control, and he'd look for ways to make my life miserable. I've seen what he does to other people when he's out for revenge."

They've never had such an intimate conversation before, although Claire has known since the moment she first met Jarrod what he's like. She wouldn't go near the man alone, as his eyes can never help but stray across her petite figure, even though she always wears black to camouflage her curves. It's doubly uncomfortable since he makes no effort to hide it from his wife, and he exudes the kind of malevolent, sadistic control that scares Claire more than anything. Therefore, she understands exactly why Elizabeth drinks to excess and wants to go easy on her. The sight of the woman standing there, so vulnerable, her heavy makeup dripping down her cheeks, makes something twist in Claire's heart. Impulsively, she goes across and puts her arms around Elizabeth, who relaxes into her hug for a few moments, before she stiffens and pulls away. "Will you listen to me," she says, her voice dripping with self-contempt. "Stood here complaining about my fortunate life and the husband who makes it all possible."

Claire watches the shutters close, one by one, across Elizabeth's face, and realizes she's stepped over some kind of line. It's too late to go back. She picks up her bag. "I'd better get to the arena," she says. "I've got two spin classes this morning."

Elizabeth says nothing as they walk to the door. "See you next week," Claire says breezily, heading to her Camry. Elizabeth shuts the door behind her.

Claire drives slowly along the manicured driveway, waiting for the large iron gates to open and let her through. She glances back at the huge house in her rear-view mirror, as the gates slide closed, and she's barely halfway along the cul-de-sac when her phone pings. She glances at it, sees it's a text from Elizabeth, and pulls over to read it.

> We're not getting the results I want.
> I'm sorry, but I'm going to look for
> another trainer. Thanks for your help.

Claire sighs. It's a relief, really. She'll miss the money but at least now she can stop making herself go to that house, swallowing down bile at the thought of being trapped inside, with Elizabeth and Jarrod and their thinly disguised malice toward one another. It's making her remember things she's worked for a long time to forget.

chapter three

LENNY

L enny waits by the front door, dangling his car keys impatiently. As usual, the morning school run is turning into a shit-show. Jake had refused to get up, chucked a tantrum over not having Coco Pops for breakfast, and wouldn't comb his hair. Meanwhile, Emily, usually more compliant, did all of these things, then burst into tears when she realized she'd forgotten to do her spelling homework, insisting she had a tummy ache until Lenny spelled out each word for her. Neither had asked where Claire was, well used to her early morning absences, but Emily had mentioned the school assembly that afternoon, saying she hoped Claire would come . . . which was lucky, as Lenny had totally forgotten about it and therefore Claire had no inkling it would be happening.

Another fail, Lenny thinks, grimacing as he calls their names again. It's only Tuesday but already he can't wait for the school week to be over. When he'd agreed to take on the role of main child-carer, he'd had no idea of the challenges he'd face. While the twins were babies, he'd adjusted to the lack of sleep a lot more easily than Claire, who'd struggled with post-partum depression for well over a year. The eventual solution had suited them both, allowing Claire an escape route to sanity and work, and Lenny an excuse not to go back to bartend-ing, which he'd begun to hate with a passion. But the sleepless babies had been nothing compared to the rage of two maraud-ing toddlers, who would not listen to anything he wanted from them, whether he pleaded, shouted, or, on occasion, cried. As soon as he'd figured out he could bribe them with sugar and television, he'd used that for a while, until his mum realized how much he was struggling and volunteered to help him out. By then there was no other way of giving him any respite, as Claire had built up an extensive client list and a busy timetable of fitness classes at the arena, and he couldn't ask her to step back when he didn't even know what he wanted to do.

He drums the car keys against his leg and yells again for the kids to hurry up, aware that he's kidding himself, as always. He knows exactly what he wants to do: it's just that there aren't many openings for out-of-practice cover-band singers, and his band had stopped picking up regular gigs some time ago. The one small light on the horizon is the reunion on Friday. It had been his old friend Dave Palmer's idea, and their old drum-mer Fletcher had jumped on board too. It had given them an excellent excuse to catch up regularly after the demands of family had meant they'd all drifted apart over the last few years. They'd even found a new bass guitar player, Eddie, a parent at the kids' school, who had a friend working in management at the city casino complex. This mate, Baz, had promised to come along and check them out, with an eye on a regular slot at the new, much-feted microbrewery that would be open by Christmas. So the Oceanside Bar had been hastily booked and the tickets had quickly sold out. They've been rehearsing for weeks, and it was pure hedonistic fun, to begin with, but as the date has drawn closer there have been more nerves and frayed tempers from all of them, and Lenny knew he wasn't the only one desperately hoping they could get the casino gig and earn some money while playing regularly again.

The white van is still parked outside the house opposite, but the doors are shut. He stands by the front door and yells, "Come on guys, we're gonna be late," and a curtain twitches in the front room of the house opposite. The next moment the girl he'd seen early this morning is sashaying over. She wears loose jeans now, with turn-ups and a crop top that shows her midriff—and there's a large stud in her belly button and another smaller one in her nose. Her accessories are youthful, but close up she's older than he'd first thought: there are a few laughter lines around her eyes. Late twenties or early thirties, he'd say if he had to guess. Similar to himself and Claire.

"Hey, neighbor," she says, with a shy wave.

"Hey," Lenny says warmly, "good to meet you. You're unpacked already?" He nods to the van.

"Yeah." She follows his gaze. "Didn't bring much." She bites her lip and waits, leaving him searching for conversation.

"Where've you come from?" he asks.

"New Zealand, little town on the North Island. We're new to Australia—Gareth's got a job here."

Lenny tries to detect a twang in her accent, but it's almost indiscernible.

"Oh, yeah, whereabouts?" he asks. "It's somewhere I've always wanted to go—my wife's a Kiwi too—but we haven't made it yet." Just as he says the words, Jake and Emily appear.

"Haven't made what?" Emily frowns.

"A trip to New Zealand."

"Oh." She looks confused. "Dad, have you got my recorder?"

"Why would I have your recorder?"

"Daaad!" Emily runs back into the house.

"We're gonna be REALLY late," Lenny calls after her. "Jake, get into the car." To his relief, for once his son climbs in without an argument.

"I'd better let you go," the woman says.

"Yeah." Lenny smiles. "Sorry, I didn't catch your name?"

"Matilda. Call me Tilly."

"All right, nice to meet you, Tilly. Perhaps we could all grab a drink together sometime, say hello properly."

"Yeah, I'd love that. Just let me know when you're free and I'll come over." Tilly waves to Lenny and Jake and heads across the road.

Did I just invite her over, or did she invite herself? Lenny puzzles as he climbs into the driver's seat. And does she plan on excluding her partner from this get-together? A bit strange. But then again, who is he to judge the state of other people's relationships when his own is a complete disaster.

He hopes the car starts the first time this morning, as it's getting embarrassing. There's something wrong with the engine, so it makes a loud screeching noise while it warms up, meaning the whole street knows whenever he's coming and going. But Claire needs the Camry for work.

Emily finally dashes out, red-faced, recorder in hand, her once neatly tied-back hair already loose and fuzzy, as though she's been rolling around on her bed. He sighs. Reminds himself he's done his best.

"Come on, Dad," Jake grumbles. "We're gonna be really late and I won't get any time in the playground."

Lenny turns the ignition and starts the car.

chapter four

CLAIRE

I t's not ideal to cross town in rush hour, but Claire is moving against the traffic so she makes it to the arena with fifteen minutes to spare. She heads for the staff changing rooms, pushes her bag into a locker, and grabs her water bottle, towel, and her phone. As she unlocks her screen, intending to search for a playlist, she sees a brief message from Lenny.

> The twins have an assembly today.
> 2:45. Really want you to be there.
> Sorry it's late notice.

She quickly checks her schedule. She's got a private client at half-past one—which means there's no way she'll get there on time. *Shit.* It crosses her mind to send a snarky reply, but she can see how frazzled Lenny has become, trying to stay on top of the juggle, often up to his elbows in shit, sometimes literally, as Jake had been a disaster at toilet training, and still needs help keeping himself clean. It's a relief to get up early and disappear, despite the guilt of leaving them, and this was the deal: they're barely on top of the finances with the money she's making now. They live month to month, praying they'll afford the rent, eking out the grocery supplies. It's already taken its toll on their sanity, and there'd been little else on the horizon until Lenny's band decided to reunite and audition for the casino gig. It would fit perfectly with her schedule, and they're both hoping it lightens the financial load a little.

She dials Lenny's number, and he picks up in seconds. "I just got your message. Can you tell Emily I'll do my best to get there, but I have a class until two thirty so I'll be driving like a maniac and I'll probably be late."

"I'll tell her. I'm sorry, I forgot it was on, or I'd have told you earlier."

"Don't worry about it."

There's an awkward silence, familiar to both of them. Claire hesitates, about to say goodbye, when Lenny says, "We've got new neighbors. Lottie's old place."

"Oh yeah?" Claire feigns interest. She couldn't care less about the neighbors, but then Lenny adds, "She's a Kiwi, so you've already got something in common."

Claire doesn't answer, but her grip tightens on the phone.

"Claire? Are you there?"

"Yes, sorry, I . . . I have to go, okay?"

"Okay, I'll see you later then—"

She hangs up while he's still talking. Sits on the bench and puts her elbows on her knees and her head between her hands, trying to control the sudden attack of dizziness. Her mind is racing ahead to the awkward conversations about home. The questions. She's furious that just the mention of the country can do this to her.

"You all right?"

She jumps, not even realizing anyone had come in. Duncan, one of the gym managers, is watching her with concern.

"Yeah," she jumps up, grabbing her water bottle. "Just had a little dizzy spell, that's all."

"You sure you're all right to teach the class?"

"Yeah, I'll be fine." She collects her towel and heads toward the door.

"Not pregnant, are you?" he calls after her, chuckling at his own attempt at a joke.

"Dickhead," she mutters under her breath as the door closes behind her. She heads down the passageway toward the first aerobics room. Half a dozen women have gathered already, calling out greetings to her as she comes in. She acknowledges them and then busies herself with her phone, hoping to avoid conversation, her hands shaking as she sets up the class playlist.

"Let's go, ladies," she shouts, climbing on the bike, needing to work off some of the adrenaline. She pumps the pedals as the music blasts from the speakers, shouting instructions, trying to convince herself that it's purely the exertion that's making her heart pound in her ears.

In front of her, the class does its best to keep up. Sweat pours off foreheads; faces turn bright red. A couple of women at the back give up and start chatting, ignoring her when she glares at them. She shouts instructions and digs in, determined to keep up the pace, when she glances across to see a figure in the doorway, watching her. There's a voice in her head:

Ryan.

She jolts back on the seat, feet coming off the pedals as she stops abruptly, completely unaware of the entire class copying the action, staring at her and then one another, breathless and confused. A long-ago voice pierces the seal of her memories, and she can hear him so clearly, it's as though his lips are pressed against her cheek:

"I haven't seen you here before. And I know I'd remember a beautiful girl like you."

Claire quickly wipes her face with the towel she always keeps between the handlebars, and as her eyes adjust, she sees it's not Ryan by the door, but only Duncan, who had been giving her a thumbs-up but is now regarding her worriedly and holding his hands up to them all in apology. He hurries toward her. "Claire, sorry, I didn't mean to distract you," he shouts under the continued blare of music. "I was just checking you're okay."

Claire nods, but her heart is still hammering in her ears. "I'm fine," she lies, "but thanks for checking." As he leaves, she turns to the class. "Sorry about that," she says through the headset mic, "let's start again and begin to bring it down," she adds, noticing the relief on many faces as she reduces the pedaling speed.

She tries to reassure herself. It's not like it's the first time she's been triggered by someone of Ryan's build and size appearing unexpectedly, but it's been a while. The New Zealand neighbor has brought back a few unbidden memories, that's all. But nevertheless, she's angry. It was eleven years ago. Even if these people had watched the news at the time, it's most likely they wouldn't remember a goddamn thing. And she has a completely different life. A different name. As far as most people know, Lucy Rutherford has been dead for a long time.

She glances at the clock and sees she's just gone over the forty-five-minute mark. How can that be? It's like the time is draining through the fissures of her thoughts. She winds the class down as quickly as she can, and jumps off the bike, trying to avoid catching anyone's eye, suspecting that the numbers in this class are about to take a dip after this disaster of a session. She busies herself while everyone leaves and is heading for the door when Duncan reappears.

"You don't seem right today, Claire," he says pointedly. "If you need to take a rest, call in sick tomorrow. And I can get cover for your classes later too, if you need it."

"Thanks," she says, avoiding his questioning glance. "I'm feeling a bit dizzy, but I'll be okay."

"Get your iron tested," he replies. "Women often get low."

"Cheers for that," she mutters under her breath as he walks off. She thinks of actually taking up his offer, but she's only had a couple of days' sick since she started. She wants to keep moving, keep working; she doesn't want to stop, because rest does not mean the same for her as it does for other people. It means trying to bring down a nervous system that's on high alert. It means more time to think. It means contemplating her guilt about her poor mothering skills. Missing the people she's never going to see again.

And sometimes, in the very worst moments, it means thinking about Ryan.

chapter five

Once back home, Lenny races around tidying up as best he can. The agent is due at eleven, but when the doorbell goes at twenty-to, he curses, sure she's turned up early to catch him out.

But when he opens the door, he finds Saskia standing there.

"I didn't see you at school drop-off this morning," she says. She looks gorgeous, as usual, long wavy auburn hair falling loose around her shoulders, vivacious green eyes, and big dimples in her apple-cheeked smile. She wears one of her flowing patterned skirts with a turquoise-and-white tie-dyed T-shirt and a chunky brown belt. A waft of her perfume winds around him.

"I had to race off," he says. "Rent inspection." He waves his hand toward the house's interior. "Always a bloody nightmare," he adds.

"I can help, if you like," she says, walking inside before he can stop her. Across the road, he spots Tilly in her carport, wiping down a small table. She's stopped to openly watch him, her head tilted quizzically to one side. He quickly shuts the door.

"I'll clean up some of the kitchen for you," Saskia says. "But first you have to kiss me."

Lenny lets out a short, embarrassed laugh, but stalls. This doesn't feel right in the house, even though it had been Claire's idea to have an open marriage. He still can't believe it's come to this. Things had imploded after the kids had come along, but it had taken Lenny a couple of years to realize the problem ran a lot deeper than the twin babies who kept them up all night and never coordinated their sleep patterns. He'd thought Claire was pushing him away because of exhaustion, until one night she'd screamed at him to stop pestering her for sex, and they'd stood on opposite sides of their bedroom, reeling and breathless, until Claire admitted she didn't want to be intimate anymore. There'd followed weeks of tense discussions alternating with uncomfortable silences, until Claire had suggested an open marriage so they could both be together for the kids. Lenny had agreed in theory, unable to imagine how that would work, and hoping time would turn her around. But instead, his wife seemed increasingly determined to avoid him as much as possible. Even though they still shared a bedroom with two single beds pushed close, because there was no spare room, and they didn't want to put the twins together where they could mess around and wake each other, Claire would usually wait until Lenny had gone to sleep before she came in, and then she'd be up and out to work before he was awake.

The impasse continued until six months ago, when he'd met Saskia. They'd flirted over school drop-offs and pickups for most of the kids' kindergarten, and he'd discovered she was co-parenting with a jealous ex who had made all her previous boyfriends' lives miserable. He'd slowly revealed his own situation, and Saskia had propositioned him with a no-strings relationship. Nevertheless, he'd felt so guilty after their first kiss that it had taken a while before they'd gone any farther, but for the last couple of months, Saskia has been his secret girlfriend, sneaking around for sex during school hours. However, despite their agreement, he still hasn't worked up the courage to tell Claire what's happening. The confession sits like a stone in his windpipe, refusing to budge, as he fears the conversation will be a catalyst for changes he's not sure he's ready for. Because while he likes Saskia a lot, in truth there's been more than one occasion when they've been naked in bed, and he's found himself wondering what the hell he's doing and thinking longingly of his wife.

Saskia comes across to Lenny and kisses him. "Close your eyes, Bob," she says to the lizard behind him, before she moves his hands onto her breasts.

He laughs. "Seriously? The agent will be here in fifteen minutes. It's housework only right now or I'm going to get evicted."

"All right then, spoilsport," she says, grabbing a tea towel, clearing the draining board while filling him in on a playground ruckus between two of the dads who had almost come to blows over a bullying incident.

"Can't say I'm sorry I missed it," Lenny is replying, wiping the dining table down just as the front doorbell chimes.

"That'll be the agent," he says, hurrying to answer it.

As he opens the door, the woman on the other side has her hand poised by the lock, a set of keys dangling from her fingers. "Hello, Lenny, I wasn't sure if anyone was here."

"Hi, Joanna. Come on in."

Joanna steps inside, her eyes already scanning the hallway for signs of wear and tear. She's in her midthirties, with shoulder-length dark hair and a wispy fringe. She wears thick-rimmed purple glasses and carries a clipboard. Lenny's only met her on a couple of occasions, but she seems a lot sterner than he remembers. His heart sinks.

"How have you all been?" she asks as she walks into the living room. Then stops with an "Oh?" as she sees Saskia.

"This is my friend Saskia," Lenny says quickly.

"Claire's not here?" Joanna asks, her eyes avoiding his as she glances around.

"She's working this morning."

Joanna's eyebrows lift briefly. "All right then. I shouldn't be long." She starts snapping pictures on her phone and writing notes on her clipboard.

Saskia moves to the sofa and Lenny sits near her. They wait in silence while Joanna bustles about collecting snapshots. "Lenny," she calls when she reaches the back bedroom.

Her tone is ominous, and Lenny pulls a worried face at Saskia as he replies. "Yep. Coming."

Joanna is staring at the hole. "We told you to fix this last time, didn't we?" she says with a disapproving frown.

"Yeah, I've been meaning to, it's just . . ."

"You're not going to fix it yourself?" Joanna asks, horrified.

"Yeah, I mean I got a quote, but it was ridiculous." Lenny can feel himself bristling.

"Bad idea, Lenny. Leave it to the professionals. And the other thing . . ." she strides out of the room, clearly assuming he'll follow, and stops in front of the lizard's vivarium ". . . is this."

Lenny's heart sinks.

"You have a no-pet clause," she reminds him.

"Yeah, but . . . that's for cats and dogs." Lenny smiles at Joanna, trying to encourage her to lighten up. "Bob sits in his tank for most of the day. He's more like a fish."

"Did you ask before you got him?"

"No, but . . ."

"How long have you had him?"

"A few months. He's been great for Jake. It really calms him down when the beardie gives him a snuggle."

Joanna is still shaking her head. "I'll have to talk to the landlord," she says, making a note on her clipboard. She glances up. "There are so many people on our waiting list. You don't want to end up breaching the contract."

Lenny is trying to control his temper. "Yes, Joanna," he says, and then catches Saskia's eye. She's biting her lip, and he sees the absurdity of it all, standing in front of the agent like a schoolboy in the principal's office. He swallows a smile, but too late.

Joanna frowns and turns to leave, waving her hand at him dismissively. "All right, all right, have a good laugh about it. You won't find it so funny when we serve you your notice."

She's heading for the door and Lenny sobers fast, following her. "Hey, I'm sorry, I understand. Thanks for checking about the dragon, I really appreciate it. And I'll get the wall fixed too."

Joanna's mouth is a thin line as she turns back to him. "You have a week," she says, "and if that wall isn't fixed by then, you're officially in breach of contract. Okay?"

"Right," he says, showing her out, and shutting the door

behind her. He goes back to the lounge and throws himself on the sofa next to Saskia, leaning back, closing his eyes, and blowing out a long breath.

"She's intense," Saskia says, and he turns to see her eyes are dancing with amusement.

"Yep."

"You gonna fix that wall?"

"Doesn't sound like I have much choice."

"I have another option."

He sits up a bit. "Oh yeah?"

"Yeah. Why don't you leave the wall, screw your contract, and come and live with me?"

He gapes at her, as she watches him intently, no amusement anymore, only hope in her expression.

"Sask," he begins, "I can't just . . ."

He watches her face drop and feels desperate but annoyed too. Why is she asking this, when they've already agreed that the situation works for them both. He can't just leave Claire and the kids. Claire might not be emotionally available but she's been doing some heavy lifting to keep the family together and a roof over their heads. She's a good mum, and if he could just pry open the part of her that she's locked away, then perhaps they'd still have a chance.

As though Saskia can read his mind, she says, "Are you gonna live in a loveless marriage forever, Lenny?"

It stings, and he wants to deflect the pain. "It's not that, it's the kids . . ." he begins.

"The kids can come with us. Claire barely spends any time with them anyway. You can even bring Bob," she adds, humor flaring in her eyes then fading when he doesn't respond.

"But Sask," Lenny says pleadingly, "we agreed that the reason this worked was because it didn't cause massive ructions. You've said yourself that Jamie can't cope with the jealousy when there're other men around your boys. And my agreement with Claire is to have an open marriage, not to end it."

"I know what I said," Saskia strikes back, her eyes gleaming. "But I don't want to stay in the same situation forever. This was all fine while we were having fun, but . . ."

"You're not having fun anymore?" Lenny asks.

Saskia bites her lip. "I love you, Lenny."

He sits back, stunned.

"I want you to be lying in bed with me every night," she says quickly, as though her confession has broken a dam and now the words are tumbling out. "I want to see you when I first wake up in the morning. I want a proper relationship. I want to deal with Jamie once and for all, otherwise, his jealousy is going to control the rest of my life. I might as well have stayed married to the idiot, if that's the case."

They stare at one another for a moment. "Jeez, Sask, I didn't realize—"

"Do you love me, Lenny?" she interrupts.

"I . . . I . . ." He can't finish the sentence.

"Well," she gets up quickly, her gaze averted now. "I guess that's it then." She hastily wipes the tears from her cheeks. "I thought we were on the same page, but now I understand. I'm just your bit of fun."

"Sask," Lenny jumps up, grabbing her arm. "Wait! It's not that! The time I spend with you is amazing, but I just didn't think it was going this way. So I haven't even allowed myself to imagine it." He can feel himself getting emotional. "I haven't let myself love you, because I never thought you wanted more than a casual thing. So I . . . I don't know how I feel, but I know I don't want us to be over like this. You understand me, and you help me lighten up and make me laugh like no one else. But you've gotta give me a minute to think about this before you decide how I feel, okay?"

She turns, her eyes searching his as though she's trying to read the truth. "All right," she says softly. "I understand. Think about it. Imagine a future with me. Allow yourself to find out if you love me. And then let me know."

She hurries to the front door and lets herself out before Lenny can catch up with her. He stands there, his head spinning, watching her racing down the path to her parked car, but only once the vehicle moves does he see that Joanna is standing by Tilly's door. Both women's arms are folded, watching him curiously. His face burns as he turns away.

chapter six

CLAIRE

By the time Claire gets to the school hall, she can hear kids singing. She tries to go unobtrusively through the double doors, but heads still turn momentarily, even some on the stage, and she winces. She double-checks that Emily isn't among the performers and then searches the room for Lenny and the kids. The entire school is taking part in the assembly, and with everyone in the same blue-and-gray uniform, it's almost impossible to see the twins, but then she spots Jake's spiky hair in the midst of a row of first-years. Lenny is in the front row of the chairs set out for parents, and she catches his eye.

"Did I miss it?" she mouths to him.

"No," he mouths back, and she breathes a sigh of relief. It's the worst feeling in the world when the kids are disappointed in her missing something important to them, but, thanks to her work commitments, it happens all too often.

She spots Lydia next to Lenny, and her mother-in-law gives her a small wave. Claire smiles back, glad to see her. Soft-spoken, Lydia has a calming, supportive presence. She's never judgmental, and Claire wishes that they were closer, but understands it's her own fault they're not. Lydia has said enough for Claire to know that she would love them to be confidants. Once, when the kids were tiny, and Lydia had come to take them for a walk, she caught Lenny and Claire in an argument, and Lenny had stormed out. In the awkwardness he'd left behind him, Claire, in tears, had said to Lydia, "Your son is too good for me." And Lydia had put a hand on Claire's arm and said, "You undersell yourself, my love. He knows how lucky he is. That's why he cares so much." And then she'd taken the kids out and Claire had gone to bed and cried herself into a restless sleep.

Now, she glances at the rows of beaming family members and briefly imagines her own mother alongside Candace and Robbie among the crowd. Her mum would be anxious because she would have had to shut her shop up for an hour to attend. Candace would be ready to holler as soon as she spotted her niece and nephew, while Robbie would look half-proud, half-embarrassed to be there. But all that was just a guess based on decade-old memories: the last time she'd seen her family, her sister had been head-down in nursing textbooks and her brother was doing his homework with his headphones on so that he could watch YouTube at the same time. But they are frozen in time. She has no idea what her family are like anymore.

She bites her lip and turns her attention back to the stage, where the kindy kids are singing the story of Little Bo Peep. Her heart melts as she watches their uncertain little faces determined to do their best, while the boys playing the sheep hide at the back of the stage, giggling.

"And now," the principal says, a couple of nursery rhymes later, after the little ones have all trooped off stage, "Our year-ones will reenact the story of the Wagyl, the Rainbow Serpent."

"Long, long ago," comes a high-pitched familiar voice, and Claire's heart fills with pride as she sees Emily reading solemnly from some papers on a lectern, her hair in pigtails. Emily's classmates pile onto the stage, some holding pictures of landscapes, others hidden beneath a brightly colored length of sheeting that serves as the snake. Emily and one of her friends take turns in recounting the story, but in the moments she isn't speaking, Claire can see her daughter's eyes scanning the rows of seats at the back. Lenny waves, but Claire knows their little girl isn't searching for him. She watches Emily's anxious face— *I'm here, Emily, I'm here, look this way*—but it's only toward the end of the play that Emily finally turns toward the doorway. As soon as she sees her mother, she breaks into a broad grin and reads her last line in her loudest, clearest voice, giving her mum a small wave before they all march off the stage.

Claire bites back her emotions. No matter how little they see of one another, Emily's connection to Claire is as fierce as Claire's feelings for her daughter. Jake is such a daddy's boy that the emotional burden feels different, and Claire can keep her son happy with games and treats from the shops. But Emily has a magnetic pull toward her mother, a constant desire to lie in the crook of Claire's arm as soon as she sees her, to bring stories to her, or to climb into bed beside her. For Claire, the overwhelming love she has for the twins is agonizing. She often tries to direct her daughter's gaze elsewhere. *I'm not safe*, she wants to tell her. *Bad things happen when I'm around. Go to your dad and stay away from me.*

The feelings had flooded her from the moment they were born. The pregnancy had been hard, and she'd been warned and prepared for ambivalent feelings toward her babies, who had spent the last few months sucking all the energy from her body, absorbing every bit of her strength into their growing little frames. However, when first one and then the other was held up to her and laid on her chest in the operating theater, she'd had a rush of protective love so fierce, so primal, that she'd almost snarled at the nurses who came to take them and weigh them. On Lenny's face she'd seen nothing except benign wonderment, while her blood coursed with fear as much as joy, as she instantly understood the enormity of her power and control over them. Hours later, as they lay helpless in her arms, she'd had the first impulse to get away; to remove them from her before she was responsible for something terrible happening to them. Because these perfect children could not belong to her, the woman who'd left a trail of broken lives without meaning to and caused unimaginable pain. *I don't deserve you*, she'd thought as she looked at these tiny, innocent, perfect little beings, and the idea began to goad her, repeating in an endless loop as her mind started to fracture through lack of sleep and the anxious first days of motherhood. The closer she tried to pull her babies to her while she put those thoughts from her mind, the more she became aware of something bestial, reawoken and prowling inside her. Her warring instincts of love and terror screamed at her to protect them from the danger she might bring. And as she suffered and struggled in those first months, she'd realized:

one part of her had known it would be like this. It was why she hadn't wanted children. It was too much of a risk. She'd made a terrible mistake, and now she couldn't undo it.

There'd been a dark, sludgy six months ending up with a trip to the doctor and sleeping pills. The mention of postpartum depression. A referral to a counselor. She'd tried to find a way to talk without revealing anything of her personal history, ending up saying that for some reason she was having flashbacks to a past trauma. An *assault*, she'd called it, although the word felt way too small and mild to encompass what she'd really experienced, and the guilt she'd carried ever since. The counselor had explained that new motherhood was often a trigger for unresolved trauma to rear its head. She'd added PTSD to the list of diagnoses and suggested regular sessions might be valuable, but Claire had never gone back. Instead, she'd tried to accustom herself to the unexpected intrusions of unwanted memories. And, mostly, it had worked. Except when Lenny got too close to her. She couldn't stand the hurt in his eyes when she flinched at his touch, but she didn't want his hands on her either. So she'd flung the open marriage suggestion at him one night, half-hating herself for it, but once it was out there she didn't want to take it back. It had felt like an escape. A way to mitigate the situation without completely losing her family.

While she's been lost in thought, the assembly has progressed, and another group of half a dozen children has filed onto the stage. Jake stands among the line of kids, as the tallest boy says, "This week it's Grandparents Day."

The girl beside him adds, "So some of us asked our grandparents about their lives."

"My granddad was an opera singer," says the smallest girl shyly. "And he once sang in Paris."

"My granddad fought in Vietnam," says the bespectacled boy beside her. "And he won a medal."

Jake steps forward. Lenny has spiked his hair for the occasion, and he wears the T-shirt they'd got him at Christmas with Bob's picture on it and writing above it that says, *My beardie is my bestie*. "My nanna was a dancer," he says, beaming. "And she was in a music video with Boy George."

Claire sees Lenny and Lydia going red with laughter, chuckling behind their hands. As the assembly finishes and they make their way over, Claire looks quizzically at Lydia. "Boy George?"

"Well, he had to have something to say," she says merrily. "And you know I did dance on *Countdown*. Besides, I didn't think that 'my Nanna was a hippy who lived in a caravan for a decade' would quite cut the mustard."

Claire has always admired the unselfconscious way her mother-in-law walks through life. Today, Lydia's wearing a long, flowing gypsy skirt and her heavily tanned, freckled skin is highlighted by the crisp whiteness of her floaty white top. Her shoulder-length auburn hair is pushed off her face by a bright turquoise scarf with a sea-shell pattern on it. For ten years, Lydia has been all warmth and love, but Claire is still reticent, knowing Lydia might well have questions that Claire doesn't want to answer.

Lenny joins them, followed quickly by Emily, who flings her arms around her mother's waist. "You made it! Did you see me? Did I do good?"

Claire beams down at Emily. "You were great. Well done, honey. Maybe we should get you a milkshake on the way home."

Jake arrives in time to add, "And me?"

Claire laughs and ruffles his hair. "And you, of course. Well done. Have you both had a good day?" The kids nod and chatter away as they leave the hall, which is good because it stops the awkwardness with Lenny. Claire can sense his eyes on her, watching her. For some reason, it's making her even more nervous than usual.

Eventually, she turns to him. "How'd the inspection go?"

Lenny grimaces. "I've got a week to fix the hole. And she wants us to get rid of Bob."

Jake's face crumples. "You won't, Dad, will you?" he begs.

"Nah," Lenny laughs, "but we might have to hide him in the attic."

Claire breathes a sigh of relief as Jake's meltdown is averted, and he runs off to play with a friend.

"Oh hey, Claire."

Claire turns to see Saskia Adams regarding her. "Hey," she says awkwardly. Saskia's interest in Lenny has been obvious before, but from the intense glances between them today, it's suddenly clear that something is going on between them. Her stomach responds to the insight with a series of griping pains, leaving her giddy. Of course this was going to happen one day, but now it's right in front of her she's not sure she's ready. She studies them both and Lenny's face flushes in response. He can't even look her in the eye. She wonders how far it's gone already: Are they in love? Does she even have the right to ask after giving him permission to look elsewhere?

"Billy did well," she says quickly to Saskia, desperate to cover her consternation before it completely overtakes her.

"Yes. He did. Are you going to Lenny's gig on Friday?"

"Not sure yet. You?"

"Oh, I'll be there, supporting the band," Saskia says, her eyes on Lenny. Then, "Sorry, I've got to be going." And she hurries away.

"What's wrong with her?" Lydia asks. Then she glances from Claire to Lenny and her easy expression falters. Claire isn't sure how much Lydia knows about the current state of their marriage, but Lydia looks troubled as she turns to the twins. "Hey, kids, do you have stuff on the classroom walls?"

"I do," Emily says immediately, and Jake adds, "Me too."

"Want to show me?" she says, holding her hands out to them and letting them lead her away.

Lenny and Claire watch them leave. Neither speaks for a moment, then Lenny takes a big breath.

"We need to talk . . ." he says quietly.

Claire spins to face him, searching his eyes, hating what she sees there. "Not here, Lenny," she snaps.

Lenny runs a hand across his face. "I know."

He stares at her desperately, and she can see the pleading in his expression. *Help me out here, Claire. I'm lost.*

She doesn't know if she has any right to be furious with him, but she is. So she says nothing.

He looks toward the classrooms. "Mum's already asked if I want her to take the kids for a bit and give them some tea. Can you come home so we can have a chat?"

Claire hesitates, instantly wanting to avoid this, since she's dreading what he might say—but that look between him and Saskia will haunt her now until she knows what's going on. "All right. I have another class tonight, but Duncan's already offered to cover it." She feels sick. Have they finally reached the moment Lenny tells her he's leaving—or asks her to go? She's always known he wouldn't stay forever. Perhaps this will make it easier on all of them.

So why does it hurt so much?

"Right," Lenny says nervously. "I'll go and ask Mum to take the kids, and I'll meet you at home." He begins to walk toward the classroom.

"Give her some money to get them both a milkshake," Claire calls after him, and he raises a hand to show he's heard. As he hurries away, Claire's aware of her heart straining, urging her to follow. But her feet stay planted firmly on the ground.

chapter seven

LENNY

As Lenny drives home, his car following Claire's, he's desperately trying to figure out how they can have this conversation without it turning heated and one of them walking out. He briefly thinks of turning the car around, heading for the beach or the pub, taking time out from everyone else's emotional demands. But the opportunity to talk to Claire like this, alone, doesn't come around often, so he grips the wheel harder, and works on his opening gambit.

At home, as they get out of the vehicles, the house opposite stands quiet, and the white van has gone. Nevertheless, he's aware of the new neighbors. In front of them, he feels self-conscious and exposed, and he's not sure why.

Ahead of him, Claire hurries into the house. He follows, and as soon as he's closed the door behind them, she turns to him. "It's okay, Lenny, we made an agreement. You've done nothing wrong. So if you and Saskia have something going, then let's talk about it."

Lenny goes to the sofa and slumps onto it, head in his hands, trying to calm himself. He's aware of Claire coming across to sit beside him. Waiting.

"I—" she begins. But he can't take anymore.

"Can you stop with the sanctimonious bullshit, Claire," he snaps.

She falls silent.

He gets up, walks toward the kitchen, starts emptying the dishwasher. Realizes what he's doing. Comes to sit back down. Looks straight at Claire.

"If it were just me, I would leave," he says, keeping a steady gaze on her. "Not because I don't love you, but because you've built a wall around yourself and I'm sick and exhausted of trying to climb over it. I accept that, for whatever reason, you can't work through anything with me. You're unreachable. And you don't love me enough to try."

"Lenny, that's not—"

He cuts across her, too angry to hear it. "It's been over two years," he says, "since we even tried . . ." He falters. "Saskia wants to be with me, I like her a lot and she doesn't push me away. But . . ."

"The kids, I know," she finishes for him, biting her lip. "I'm sorry, Lenny."

"Yes, the kids," he says in frustration, "but what about *us*, Claire? We had something so special, I still can't believe it's come to this. Do you really feel so little for me that you don't care if I leave?" He leans forward. "I still don't fucking get it."

Her mouth opens, and he waits, praying that she'll spill

whatever she's been clutching so tightly for years. That his mention of the past might have jogged her memories back to those early months of pure happiness: the lazy mornings in bed and evenings out dancing, and the impromptu trip to Vegas and that little wedding chapel where he'd promised to love her forever.

Instead, the doorbell rings.

"Ignore it," he says as Claire's eyes drift toward the hallway.

They stare at each other for a moment, hoping that whoever it is will go away. But then there's another ring and a voice calls, "Anyone there?"

"Oh for fuck's sake," he hisses. "It's the new woman from across the road."

Something shifts in Claire's expression. She covers it quickly, but she'd seemed uncomfortable.

"Hello!" a voice calls from outside. "Anyone home?"

"She'll know we're home, the cars are outside," Lenny says wearily. "I'll try to get rid of her." He gets up and goes down the hall.

He opens the door to find Tilly wearing a wide, lipsticked smile, clutching a bouquet of red gerberas. A bottle of wine pokes out of her large shoulder bag.

"Hey neighbor," she says, her voice light as she steps inside and heads down the hall. "So I'm almost unpacked and that means it's time for a celebration!" He follows her back down the hallway and hears her say, "Oh, hello."

Claire stands up slowly, her expression wary. Tilly stops for a moment, and the women assess each other. Then Tilly hurries across and proffers the flowers. "You must be Claire," she says. "I've been waiting to meet you all day."

"You have?" Claire says as she hesitantly takes the bouquet.

"Oh yeah, after Lenny's warm welcome this morning I knew straight away that we would all be great friends. I was chatting to Joanna about you earlier on—she's our agent too—and she said you guys are always so lovely that she knew we'd get on well."

"Did she?" Claire responds, smiling politely. Every time she's met Joanna the woman has been curt to the point of rudeness; she can't imagine her saying any such thing, but perhaps Tilly is trying to be kind. "Thanks for these," she adds, avoiding Lenny's eye. He knows she hates fresh-cut flowers. Early on he'd bought her a bouquet of roses, and she couldn't even take them from him when he'd held them out to her. Bad memories, she'd told him. He'd mentioned it to his mother, who'd reminded him that she'd become flower phobic for a time after Lenny's father died, after receiving so many that the house was filled with a pungent aroma that turned quickly from pleasant to sickly as the bouquets wilted in the summer heat. They'd concluded that it might be part of the childhood trauma Claire couldn't talk about—so he hadn't asked. He just never bought her flowers again.

Tilly is glancing around the living room, still talking. "So, this is a lovely house. I'm sorry Gary isn't here, he's on the phone with the office. Work never stops, you know."

"What does he do?" Claire asks.

"Building contractor. Oversees projects. Super boring." Tilly grabs the bottle from her bag. "The flowers are for you, but I thought we could share the wine. You got some glasses?" She looks between them, then seems to sense the lack of enthusiasm. "Sorry, have I interrupted something? I won't stay long but at least let's have a toast to new friends!"

Lenny and Claire exchange glances of resignation as Lenny goes across to the kitchen cupboard and hunts for glasses, unable to remember the last time he'd drunk wine at home.

Tilly hasn't stopped talking. "When I bumped into Lenny this morning and he was so friendly, I was so grateful. You never know what the neighbors are going to be like when you move to a new place, do you? Oh, and who's this?" Tilly strides over to Bob's vivarium. "Oh my god, it's a little lizard," she says. "How cute is he?"

"It's a bearded dragon," Lenny says, pulling the cork on the wine.

"And you can keep them like this?" Tilly asks. "Is it legal?"

Lenny is amused by her directness, and he can see Claire is too. "Yes, it's fine. Bob is captive-bred, we didn't take him out of the wild."

Tilly peers through the glass as the lizard watches her with a haughty sidelong stare. "Isn't it hard to keep them alive?"

Lenny hands her a glass of wine. "They can live for a long time, if you know how to care for them. Ten years or more. It's my son's, he's only eight but he'll probably be taking it with him when he leaves home."

"*Your* son's?" Tilly asks curiously, the question clear.

"Our son's," Lenny says, reddening. He hands the other glass of wine to Claire. "Shall we take these outside?"

Claire studies the drink as though considering whether to have it. "Okay," she says. "Good thing I canceled my class." The women follow Lenny through the house and out of the patio doors.

"You're a student?" Tilly asks as they take their seats on the veranda, with its charming view of the dirty plastic swing set and deconstructed sandpit, its contents spattered across the grass.

"I teach fitness classes at the local sports center," Claire says.

Tilly looks her up and down admiringly. "Ah, I thought you were fit." She pats her own flat stomach. "I could do with getting in shape. I might have to come along."

"Your husband looks like he spends plenty of time at the gym," Lenny cuts in.

"Oh, Gary isn't my husband, I've only been with him for a few months. This is our first place together," she says, "and between you and me, I'm not sure if we'll work out. He's very . . ." She pauses for a moment, as though summoning the right word. "Intense," she states finally.

Claire leans forward, frowning. "But you still moved in with him?"

Tilly laughs. "Not as such—I got a new place and he tagged along with me. Still, he makes me feel a bit safer at night, so he has his uses."

Claire catches Lenny's eye, echoing his surprise, and then laughs so unguardedly that Lenny is taken aback. As he watches the women talk, he relaxes despite himself. It appears that Claire has forgotten their troubles too, while Tilly is a charmer and doesn't let the conversation falter. She asks a lot of questions but somehow avoids the awkward ones: quizzing them about the kids, what the neighborhood is like, and where she might find work. He suddenly wants to hang on to this moment, to keep Tilly here so they don't have to return to their earlier conversation. When the wine glasses are drained, he refills them, and neither woman objects. Only when the bottle and glasses are empty, and the sun is low in the sky, does Tilly say, "Can I use your bathroom before I go?"

"Sure, I'll show you," Claire says, jumping up.

Lenny waits, listening to Tilly admiring the photos of the kids as they head through the house. Claire returns on her own and sits down opposite Lenny. "Well, she's something, isn't she," Claire laughs. "I can't remember the last time I drank two glasses of wine before dinner. I feel giddy."

Their eyes linger on one another. *God, you're beautiful, Claire*, Lenny thinks. *Even now, I don't want to imagine life without you.*

He wouldn't give the twins up for anything, but it was obvious that Claire's pregnancy had been a disaster and a catalyst for everything that followed. It wasn't planned; in fact they'd been talking about taking off and traveling for a while before Claire realized her boobs had been sore for weeks and her period was way overdue. The shock of the first pregnancy test had been jolting enough to delay a trip to the doctors until nearly twelve weeks, and by the time they had the first sonogram, the two fetuses were clearly formed. She'd been tired and sore and ill from the halfway point; then was battered by the cesarean and the constant demands of two tiny babies. By the time Lenny and Claire had emerged from their sleepless fog, the twins were toddlers, with parents who hardly recognized one another anymore. In the scramble to keep their babies alive and a roof over their heads with one income, they'd foregone all the things that had brought them together: music, nights out, lazy mornings in bed. Lenny wanted to recapture it—somehow—but Claire had already checked out. Her new role was breadwinner, and while she made an effort to attend family events and the children's school performances, she avoided one-on-one time with him at all costs. He hadn't pushed the sex for ages, because he didn't want to be a prick when she was so obviously struggling, and when he'd finally tried, pulling her close to him one night and kissing her neck, his fingers tentatively moving inside her shirt, the fallout had been devastating. Claire had shoved him away as though he were assaulting her, and in the tearful conversation that followed had confessed she felt permanently damaged and uninterested from the rigor of pregnancy and birth, which had left her with stitches and an abdominal separation that took a long time to heal. He'd offered suggestions—a counselor, taking it slowly, a weekend away—but Claire shut down every option, both that night and in the weeks and months that followed. He hadn't wanted the open marriage she proposed, but neither did he want a life without intimacy. So they'd slowly, inevitably, come to this. He's annoyed that he feels so guilty, because it isn't his fault, is it? He's tried everything.

As he thinks over their troubles, Claire surveys the garden. Lenny knows she's still aware of him watching her, and he wills her to look back at him. When she finally turns, he winks, and she smiles. His heart leaps, but then Tilly is back.

"I've been having such a great time that I've forgotten I'm going out tonight," Tilly says, her bag slung over her shoulder. "I'd better go."

They get up to show her out. "Thanks for coming," Lenny says as they follow her to the door. "Next time you'll have to tell us more about you. I feel like we've talked a lot about ourselves."

"That's okay," Tilly says cheerfully. "It's been nice getting to know you better. You're much friendlier than the last neighbors we had."

"Didn't you say you're from New Zealand?" Lenny asks as they all walk to the door. "You don't have a strong accent."

"Ah," Tilly says, staring at Claire, "I haven't lived there for a long time, but I'm from a little place called Silverlakes. It's an outer suburb of Hamilton, quite small really. I don't suppose you know it."

She gives them one final broad smile before she leaves, and Lenny turns back toward Claire, expecting to find her still amused by the unexpected events of the afternoon. But instead, just for a moment, before she locks down her expression, his wife's face is a mask of pure horror.

chapter eight

CLAIRE

"Claire . . . Claire . . . are you okay?"

Claire is lost in thoughts of the past. As Lenny moves closer, she immediately comes back to the present and takes a tiny step away from him. It's instinctive and she hopes he doesn't notice, but his expression drops into hurt and confusion, and her head spins.

Did Tilly really just say Silverlakes?

Lenny doesn't take his eyes off Claire, and she can't look away. She knows he can see through her when all she wants is to hide.

"Claire," he says again softly, and her vision spins, her head throbbing with the after-effects of the wine. She gazes at her husband, this beautiful, kind man whom she's tried her hardest to avoid for the last few years. And now, his soft, sweet voice saying her name like that, and the lulling effects of alcohol, are combining to pull down every defense she has tried to build around herself. She thinks of telling him everything. She's asked herself a thousand times how she would start the conversation. She imagines herself looking Lenny in the eye, wondering, *How can one person do so much damage?*

She opens her mouth, then closes it again. Lenny is waiting, and instead of talking, she moves toward him. Partly because at this moment she can't constrain the emotion she has been guarding for such a long time. But also because she knows that there is one thing that might make him forget about the expression he just saw on her face, and she wants to avoid the questions for as long as she can. So she leans up and kisses him.

After all this time she half expects him to push her away and demand that she explain. But he doesn't. He seizes the moment, wrapping his arms around her and kissing her with a hunger so intense that she can't catch her breath. The intensity frightens her, and suddenly she can't breathe. For a moment it's not Lenny who is holding her this tight, and the feeling twists from longing to terror. She pushes him away, much harder than she means to.

"What the hell, Claire?" Lenny gasps in shock. Then he sees her face and is instantly concerned. "Shit, are you okay?"

It's the way he says it that makes her pull back more, because he doesn't deserve this. She can't lead him on.

"I'm sorry, Lenny, I shouldn't . . ."

He looks crestfallen. "Help me out here—I don't understand."

She opens her mouth. Stops. There's a gentle whooshing in her ears. She can't think. There are too many images of Ryan rushing on her all at once: the broad grin that had lit her up to start with; and his tight grip on her hand as he pulled her through the dark. And there's someone else too: the shadow of another face that, if she lets it, will haunt her even more than Ryan.

She opens her mouth, but nothing comes out. She turns away.

Lenny sighs long and loud. "Wait here," he says, heading toward the back of the house. Moments later he returns, his phone in his hand. "Mum just sent a message. She'll be back with the kids in half an hour," he says. Then he swipes at the screen again and holds the device out to her. "I don't know what's happening with you, but you need to see this."

She takes the phone from him silently and reads the text on the screen.

> Your wife is a liar.

She scrolls backward, seeing more and more of the hateful little sentences. There are so many that her eyes blur and she has to look away.

"How long have you been getting these?" she asks, handing the phone back to him.

"A few weeks. I couldn't decide what to do about them. I didn't want to upset you. Do you know what they mean?"

She holds his gaze. She's a good liar; she's had a lot of practice. "No, I have no idea."

He swallows hard and she watches him trying to contain his emotions. "Can you sit down with me for a moment?"

She follows him through to the lounge and takes a seat beside him. He deserves to know, she thinks. She should at least try to explain. But she realizes now what she didn't at the start: the longer she left it, the harder it's become to share the details of a life that she's shut away for so long.

She can still hear Ryan's voice so clearly, and if she closes her eyes, he's there in front of her, in a tight white T-shirt that clings to his sculpted torso.

"You want to come for a drink after training?" he'd asked her, the very first time he saw her.

She's revisited that moment so often: the split second in which she could have changed her destiny by just saying no. But at the time she'd been happy to agree; the attraction sizzling between them; his white teeth gleaming as he'd grinned at her reply.

Lenny sits down and waits for her to do the same. His face is ashen, his entire body tensed as though expecting a sudden blow. In the past, when she tried to justify her decisions, and the tower of secrets she'd built in order to protect herself, part of her blamed Lenny. He'd rushed her into loving him, into living with him, into their marriage even, and certainly into the kids, which she hadn't been ready for. Still wasn't ready for, if she was honest. But she'd never doubted Lenny's fundamental goodness. He was a big-hearted man in a world of narcissism and aggression, and she'd always felt safe around him. It was a feeling that at one time she'd never thought she would have again, and she owed him a lot for that.

So what now? Should she tell him everything and warn him that the past might finally be catching up with her. That he might be in danger too?

She waits while he studies his hands, watching him mentally rehearsing his lines.

"Do you remember the first night we met?" he asks, his voice choked with emotion.

"Of course I do," she answers in a whisper, feeling her own heartbeat quickening. The redeeming part of her shitty bar job had been that every Saturday night she'd gotten to hear Lenny sing.

"I'd been working up the courage to talk to you for such a long time," Lenny says, "but then you disappeared, and I was gutted—thinking I'd missed my chance. But you'd just been off sick, and the night you came back I knew I couldn't wait any longer."

She remembers how he'd leaned across the bar with that gorgeous grin on his face, saying how glad he was to see her again. Asking if they could get together after the show.

"When you said you'd have a drink with me, I sang the whole set on a high, desperate to impress you, but also impatient for it to be over so we could talk properly. And then we stayed at the Southside retro bar till it closed, listening to Foo Fighters and Oasis and drinking beer. We were inseparable, Claire! You can't deny that. So inseparable that we were in Vegas getting married after only six months together." He glances around the house with a frown as though confused to find themselves here, all these years later. "What the hell happened to us?"

Claire can hardly look at him. That first date had been the happiest night of her life, finding this person who could finish her sentences and laugh at her jokes and understood what she was trying to say even when she bungled the words. He was so different from any man she'd ever been out with before, with his long wavy dark hair, the skinny black jeans and loose shirts that were so scruffy but somehow cool in an understated way. For weeks she had listened to him sing soppy ballads as if he believed every word, and in person, there was nothing macho about him at all. He wore his heart on his sleeve, talked about his love of animals, his voluntary work at the dog shelter, and his close relationship with his mum. And yet she felt he was the most interesting guy she'd ever met. He was strong in a way she'd hardly come across before, as his strength seemed to lie in the ability to sit comfortably in his own skin with whoever he was speaking to. It was such a relief, and a total contrast to the last man who had paid her attention, with his posturing, false bravado, and his body built for show.

"I thought I'd found my soul mate, Claire," he says, cutting through her thoughts.

She stares at him. She's told him before that she'd felt the same, but it doesn't feel fair to repeat that to him right now. Not after everything she's put him through.

Undaunted by her lack of response, he takes her hand. "I don't understand what went wrong," he continues. "But somehow we got lost among all this." He gestures around the house. "And by trying to meet the needs of those two demanding little souls who have ripped our hearts out and won't give them back."

She laughs at this, though her heart quickens at the thought of Emily and Jake, so sweet and so innocent.

"So now I need you to trust me," he says. "Please, whatever is going on, you have to let me in."

She hesitates and he presses on, as though he knows how close he is to cracking her.

"Just talk to me, Claire," he insists.

She thinks of the texts. Her growing anxiety today, and the gloating, knowing way that Tilly had said the word *Silverlakes*. The word reverberates around her skull, a goading, continual chant that pulses through her mind. But far worse than that are the memories that go with it: the darkened house; the single screech of terror before the silence was flooded with horror; the floor slick with blood.

"Claire?" Lenny's voice is pulling her back. "Claire, you've gone white. Are you okay?"

She focuses on her breathing; on squeezing her hands into fists, trying to ground herself back in the present. This is all happening too fast, and she needs more time.

"I do want to talk to you, Len," she says eventually, looking up to see him watching her with an expression that hovers somewhere between concern and fear. "I really do. But the kids will be back in twenty minutes, and your gig is in less than forty-eight hours. You've wanted this opportunity for such a long time, and you don't need this distraction right now. How about we ask your mum if she'll take the kids over the weekend and then we can really talk everything through."

He sighs. "God, I don't know if I can bear to ask Mum for another favor," he says. "But perhaps there isn't much alternative. It's just . . ." his intense gaze challenges her, "you need to tell me now if you're seeing someone else. I can't wait for three days to hear that."

"I'm not with anyone else, Lenny."

He doesn't appear convinced, until she adds, "I promise, on the kids' lives, okay?" She can see the mention of the kids persuades him. "I don't know who is sending those messages," she adds, gesturing toward the phone, "but they're just trying to cause problems. Could it be Saskia . . . ?" she adds without thinking. "Perhaps she wants you to leave me, and this is her way of pushing you into a decision."

Lenny opens his mouth as though to object but then closes

it again. "I don't know," he says. "Shit. Look, you're right, every-thing is complicated. We'll hold off until the gig is done. But after that we have to start working this out somehow, or . . ."

He trails off, and she gets up, not wanting him to see the glut of emotions that threaten to flood her. She heads for the bathroom, thinking of that stream of insidious little sentences on his phone. Has someone really discovered the truth of her past? Whatever is going on, she needs to figure it out fast, so she can decide how much danger they're in.

chapter nine

LENNY

Lenny wakes up with a rock on his chest, and it takes him a moment to realize it's anger. It's an unusual, uncomfortable feeling for him, and he rubs at the spot as he gets up and makes his coffee, hoping it will dissipate, but it doesn't.

He's not sure where the feeling has come from and who it's directed toward. Claire? Saskia? Tilly? Himself? The more he thinks about the way Claire had acted last night, the more confused he feels. She'd kissed him; she'd shown signs of opening up to him. And now he's cross with himself for letting her shut the conversation down. She'd done a good job of phrasing it to make it sound like she was doing him a favor, but this morning he's not so sure.

He tries her mobile, but it's switched off. Of course. He sighs. He's not relishing the upcoming school run. What if he runs into Saskia and she demands a decision from him? Shit, how has he gotten himself into such a mess?

He wakes the kids at seven and gets in the shower while they're hauling themselves out of bed. He's still sopping wet when he hears a shriek from the living room. "DAAAD! DAAAD!'

It's one of those wails that sends a cold shiver down his spine. He rushes into the lounge, skidding on the tiles as he drips everywhere, to find Jake with his hands on the vivarium, edging back and forth around the glass frontage as he peers inside.

"Bob's gone, Dad," Jake cries.

Lenny hurries over, trying not to let the ripple of annoyance interfere with his ability to comfort his son. "No, mate," he says, crouching down in front of the tank. "You know he likes to hide in the leaves at the back. Let's search together."

Lenny expects to spot the dragon straightaway—and isn't sure why Jake is having such trouble. Bob's not tiny anymore and his long, slender gray tail usually hangs down from wherever he's hiding. With growing horror, he realizes Jake is right. Bob isn't there.

"Did you open the vivarium?" he asks in confusion, trying to figure out what's happened.

"No, Dad, I swear," Jake says between gulping sobs.

"Hey, I'm not accusing you, I promise," Lenny says, grabbing Jake and pulling him close. "Do you know when you last saw him?"

"Yesterday. He was on the log. I forgot to say goodnight to him after Nanna's, and now he's gone," Jake wails.

"All right, well he can't have gone far." Lenny hurries around the house in confusion, as though Bob might be lurking underneath the furniture, watching them with that acerbic reptilian eye. Jake clings to him, and Lenny can feel the desperate pull in those little arms.

He thinks of calling Claire, but what's the point. Then he remembers his mum was here briefly last night too.

He rushes back to the bedroom, toweling himself off and grabbing a pair of shorts. He's dialing the number as he comes back through, his heart breaking to see Jake still searching the vivarium as though Bob might miraculously reappear.

"Morning, honey." His mum sounds tired. "Everything all right?"

"Er, kind of. We've lost the lizard. Do you remember seeing him when you dropped the kids off last night?"

"I did have a look for him, but I couldn't spot him," she answers. "I thought he'd tucked himself behind the leaves like he does when he's tired."

"Well, he's not in there now."

"That's so strange." Lydia sounds more alert. "Where else could he be?"

Lenny tries to think back over the previous day, but can't recall anything particularly unusual.

Until Tilly came.

He jolts, remembering her interest in the lizard, the way she'd peered into the cage.

"Lenny?"

He realizes he's gone silent. "Don't worry, Mum, I'm sure we'll find him if we do a good search."

"All right, well, let me know. Poor Jake."

I'm going mad, Lenny thinks as he ends the call. Why the hell would the new neighbor take the lizard?

He rechecks the hidey-holes in the vivarium, and all the corners of the house that Bob might have found. The main doors have been closed, so there's no chance he could have accidentally escaped into the garden, and the dragon is nearly full-grown, almost as long as Lenny's forearm from head to tail, so not easily missed.

He tries to put Tilly to the back of his mind, sure he's clutching at straws. But half an hour later, after he's gone into Jake's room to find him sobbing facedown on the bed, he grabs a T-shirt and doesn't bother with shoes. Outside, he jogs across the road and knocks on the front door of the house opposite. Adrenaline has pushed him this far, but it's cold outside this early, and he's shaking from a combination of both things by the time the door opens.

Up close, Gary is even taller than he'd thought, and he's wearing a singlet that shows off the impressive contours of his arms. "What can I help you with this time of the morning?" he asks Lenny pointedly, blinking sleep from his eyes and squinting in the daylight.

"Er, Tilly came around to say hello last night and took an interest in our bearded dragon—and it's gone this morning," Lenny says. He suddenly feels absurd, standing here with his accusations when the lizard is probably hiding in the house somewhere. "I just wondered if she knew anything."

"Hey, Till," the man shouts into the darkness behind him. "The neighbor wants to know if you stole his bearded dragon." He turns back to Lenny with a smirk, and Lenny stiffens. He can't tell if Gary is finding this amusing or insulting.

There are some noises from inside then Tilly appears at the door in a skimpy silky nightdress through which Lenny can make out the contours of her body. He tries not to notice that her nipples are pressing against the thin fabric as she beams at him.

"Hey, Lenny. I'm sorry you've lost the lizard. I'm sorry

but I don't know anything about it," she says with a wide, toothy smile.

Lenny looks from one to the other of them, feeling their amusement as he stands there in his rumpled T-shirt and board shorts. They wait to see what he does next, but Lenny is all out of ideas.

"All right then," he says. "Thanks anyway." He begins to walk away, feeling like a total fool.

"Have a good day," Tilly calls out behind him.

Back in the house, Jake has been watching through the front window.

"Did she have it?" he asks hopefully as soon as Lenny comes back, and Lenny's heart breaks at his son's childish expectation that if she *had* taken it, she would return it as soon as they asked.

"No," he says, and Jake's face starts to crumple. "But that's a good thing, buddy. It means he's more likely roaming the house, and I'll turn this place upside down today until I find him," he continues, envisioning his planned music practice flying out the window. But at least a dragon hunt will keep his mind off other problems.

"You won't find him," Jake says as he jumps down from the couch. "She took him." He kicks hard at the sofa.

"Hey," Lenny says desperately. "We don't know that. Let's get you ready for school, and I promise I'll spend my whole day searching. I'll even rustle up a search party if I need to—I'm sure your Nanna will help—and we won't stop until Bob is back in his vivarium. By the time you get home . . ." He hesitates, not wanting to make false promises. He's thinking of the dealer he'd bought Bob from, and how similar all the reptiles had been. Perhaps if the worst came to the worst, then a replacement might be the easiest way forward. But Christ, they were hundreds of dollars.

He's expecting Jake to push back, but the boy just stomps off, and Lenny breathes a sigh of relief. He goes to wake Emily and explains what has happened, and Emily immediately bites her lip worriedly, then gets up quickly when he tells her they're going to be late again.

They all get ready in heavy silence, with Lenny calling out the time every few minutes, cajoling them along. When he goes to grab his keys from the hook by the door, he realizes the spare set is missing. He has a quick look around before he texts Claire and his mother, asking if they'd taken them. When they both reply no, Lenny's mood takes another dive.

As he ushers the kids out of the door and helps them into the car, he glances at the house opposite, overcome by a surge of protectiveness toward his inconsolable son. Now he's remembering the big bag Tilly had brought with her, from which she'd produced the wine. It was plenty big enough for a lizard, but he still can't believe that she would have the nerve to take their pet. Surely, he's got this wrong.

He feels the first flash of anger toward Claire. He shouldn't be dealing with all this shit on his own, managing everything at home while she gets to swan in and out of the house between classes, or fobs him off in the middle of an important conversation when things get too uncomfortable.

He swallows down the irritation and gets into the car, wincing as the engine makes its usual high-pitched screech as they travel down the road toward school. He's been so lost in thoughts of the lizard and Claire that he doesn't think of Saskia until he's parking in the busy school parking lot. He helps the children out of the car and keeps his head down as he takes them quickly to their classrooms, hoping to keep a low profile. Emily sees a friend and runs ahead, but Jake is trudging behind all the way. Lenny turns to wait for him, despondent at the sight of his miserable little face.

"Hey, Lenny," a voice says close by, and he turns to see Trent, the father of Jake's buddy Reef. "Me and the missus are coming to your gig on Friday," Trent says enthusiastically. "Really looking forward to it."

"Great," Lenny says, trying his best to sound thrilled. At school, word has got around that this gig, featuring not one but two school dads, is a hot ticket. It feels like every time he's talked to someone in the last week, they've told him they're coming to see him and the band, and how excited they are. The last time he played in public he had a completely different life. In this world he's the twins' dad first and foremost, and it's both daunting and exhilarating to revisit this other part of himself and put it out there again. He'd love to stop and chat, but he's all too aware of Jake trudging ahead of him miserably, so says, "See you there," and hurries on.

They're almost to the classroom when Jake stops walking and plants his feet firmly where he stands. "I'm not going in," he says, folding his arms. "I wanna go home and find Bob."

Lenny hurries across and puts his arm around him. "No, buddy, I promise I'll look for him."

"NO!" Jake shouts and begins to run back toward the parking lot.

Every head turns, which at this time of the morning means most of the lower primary school kids, mums, and teachers are staring their way. Lenny pauses for a second, then begins to jog after his son, but Jake is going so fast that soon they are both sprinting across the grassy oval. Jake reaches the car a few seconds before Lenny, pulling repeatedly, angrily, at the door handle.

Lenny holds his hands in the air, chest heaving. "All right, mate," he says, "you can come back with me. We'll search together."

Jake seems stunned at the unexpected victory. He throws himself into the car, and Lenny has his hand on the driver's door handle when he sees Saskia's car reversing out of a parking lot space nearby. She pulls up alongside him, winds the window down, and says, "Wait a sec, Lenny," driving a short distance farther to park in a vacant space. She gets out of her car and hurries toward him. "I saw Jake racing across. What's happened?" she asks as she catches up, her eyes straying to Jake, who is lying on the back seat of the car sobbing.

"Bob's missing."

"Oh no. Jake loves him so much."

"Yep. So we're going home to conduct another thorough search." Lenny jangles his keys, keen to get going, aware there are other parents coming into the parking lot, openly watching them.

"Let me come and help you look," Saskia says, putting a hand on Lenny's arm. He flinches, moving away a little, hoping she won't see it as rejection. "I think it's better if it's just the two of us but thank you. Don't you have to drop your boys off anyway?" He looks over her shoulder at her car.

"Oh—no. I was almost home but then I found their water bottles on the back seat, so I've just taken them in." She waits, as though expecting Lenny to say something more.

"Why can't she help, Dad?" Jake grumbles. "You said we need a search party."

Lenny sucks in a sigh and tries a smile instead. "If you're sure," he relents, hoping she'll sense his discomfort and back off.

"Of course. I'll follow you home," Saskia replies immediately, heading over to her car.

Lenny looks helplessly at Jake, who is now sitting up and wiping his nose with his hand. "Daaad," he complains as soon as Lenny catches his eye. "Come on."

By the time they're halfway home, Jake is snuffling in his hands, and as they pull onto the drive, he's openly sobbing. Lenny comes around to the passenger door and picks him up, which he does so rarely these days, carrying him inside. Jake wraps his arms tightly around Lenny's neck, and they sit on the sofa and settle for a moment.

"All right then, bud, let's turn this place upside down," he says. He kneels in front of the sofa, peering under it, but then, from behind him, Jake says, "Dad, Dad . . ."

Lenny looks up, just as Saskia joins them. Jake is pointing to the vivarium, where Bob sits on his branch as though nothing has happened.

"What the fuck—?" Lenny says without thinking, causing an extra "*Dad!*" from Jake.

"You found him already?" Saskia asks, giving Jake a beaming smile.

"We didn't even have to look," Lenny says in confusion. "He was already there."

They move over to the vivarium and get Bob out to check he's okay. Jake strokes him and Bob endures it stoically. Lenny stands, hands on hips, contemplating the size of the reptile, almost the length of his forearm from head to tail. There's no way they wouldn't have spotted Bob this morning if he'd been in the vivarium or the house. Something very strange is going on.

"I'd better get going then," Saskia says. "I'm really glad he's okay, Jake." As Lenny watches, she briefly strokes Jake's hair. *Like a mother would*, Lenny thinks uncomfortably, following her to the front door while Jake stays behind, clutching Bob.

"Thanks for trying to help," he says as he follows Saskia down the hallway.

"No problem." Saskia turns and stares at him intently. "You know I would do anything for you."

She is gone before he can reply, and he closes the door, calling to Jake that they'd better get back to school. But then his step falters, as he catches sight of the row of hooks on the wall. The spare keys have miraculously reappeared. Just like Bob.

chapter ten

CLAIRE

By the time Claire finishes her second aerobics class of the morning, there are two missed calls on her phone and a text from Lenny:

> Bob's back, safe and sound.
> False alarm.

Tired and relieved, she orders a cup of tea at the little indoor café at the arena and takes it with her to sit on a bench outside in the spring sunshine. Her body aches from spending all morning exercising with tense, weary muscles. She'd hoped that the rigors of work would force her to set aside her worries, but the harder she tries to stay focused, the louder her thoughts intrude, demanding she pay attention.

She'd been shaken, finding out Bob had been gone, listening to Lenny's suspicions and reliving Tilly's quick exit, picturing her hiding the creature under her jacket while inwardly gloating at them behind that too-wide, gleeful grin. Claire's fury had grown as the morning progressed, meaning she barked commands at her classes and pushed them to their limits, only satisfied when she saw them drenched with sweat and shaking from exertion. At least the heady sense of control had helped her to block out the image of her son's woebegone face. Jake loved that little reptile like his best friend, and she could feel his distress and worry as though it were her own.

She texts a quick reply to Lenny, then considers the other missed number, working up the courage to return the call. She's about to reopen a wound she'd hoped she'd closed forever, but she also needs answers, or the fears will overtake her. So she dials the number and waits.

Mary-Rose picks up after a few rings. "Well, hello, my dear! It's been a while, now, hasn't it," she says, and it's such a relief to hear her voice, with its strange blend of Irish lilt and Kiwi inflections. If it hadn't been for Mary-Rose, Claire doubts she would have survived any of the trauma of eleven years ago. It was Mary-Rose who'd helped her with the police visits and the court case, as well as the pointed glances and silences from her own community—even some of those closest to her. Mary-Rose might have been her support worker to begin with, but by the end, she'd felt like one of Claire's closest friends. And she was the only person from Claire's past who knew where she was now.

"It's really good to hear your voice," Claire says. "Thanks for calling me back so quickly. I'm sorry to bother you, but there's been a few strange things happening at home—and I know I'm probably just being silly, but this is what I've always dreaded . . . him finding me again."

"It's all right," Mary-Rose says gently. "I'm glad you called. Why don't you start by telling me what's happened?"

Claire explains about the texts on Lenny's phone, the new neighbors, and Tilly's mention of Silverlakes. She thinks about adding the story of Bob's mysterious, temporary disappearance but worries she might sound unhinged.

Once she's finished, there's an extended pause on the other end of the line, as though Mary-Rose is weighing her words. Claire expects to be told not to worry, but instead, Mary-Rose says, "Well, I can understand why you're unsettled. It's all a little bit unusual, isn't it—especially those messages to your husband. And your new neighbor mentioning Silverlakes out of the blue like that. But the most important thing to remember is that Ryan's never getting out of jail," Mary-Rose adds gently.

Claire feels her breath catch at the voicing of his name. "I keep telling myself that but I need to know for certain that he's still in there. Please, could you check for me?"

"Of course," Mary-Rose says. "I'll make a few calls today. But remember, the judge said he wouldn't be released for a very long time, if at all."

"I know. But what if he's persuaded someone that everything was my fault? His family probably still hates me, and he's a master manipulator. I'm sure he knows people who aren't afraid of breaking the law for revenge. Perhaps Tilly is a relative of his . . . ?"

Mary-Rose cuts across her, decisive and businesslike. "Well, let's get on and check this out so we can put your mind at rest. I'll need some names, and I'll investigate for you. I've already got your address. What's the house number for your neighbors?"

"Fifteen."

"And it's Tilly and Gary?"

"Yes. I'm not sure of their last names."

"I'll call back if I need them. I might not. Let me see what information I can get, and meanwhile, don't panic. This could all be a storm in a teacup. It's highly unlikely that after all this time—'

"I know," Claire cuts in. "I realize I sound paranoid . . ."

"No, it's not that at all. I just want to reassure you. When I told you to call if anything bothered you, I meant it. And you've not contacted me for years, so this has obviously thrown you."

"There's something else," Claire says. "Can you check on my mum and Candace and Robbie?"

As she talks, Claire becomes aware of a sleek black Audi pulling up in front of her on the footpath. It's about ten meters away across the paved, pedestrianized area in front of the health club, and the windows are blacked out, so there's no way of seeing who's inside. Her colleagues would probably go over to tell the driver it was a no-stopping area, but Claire stays where she is.

"Can I just ask," Mary-Rose continues, "have you ever told anyone over there about what happened, besides Devon?"

"No."

"Not even your husband?"

Claire pictures Lenny with a crushing wave of guilt. "No," she says softly, her eyes on the stationary car, "it was easier that way."

The Audi is still there, and suddenly she wonders if the person inside is watching her. Why does she suddenly feel that the car is familiar? She shifts uneasily, aware she's sitting out here, exposed, talking about the man who had once stalked her for months, and there is a car right here with someone hidden inside. A moment later she gets a rush of terror and jumps to her feet. "Thanks for your help, Mary-Rose," she says hastily. "I have to go."

"Hang on, you sound spooked. Are you okay?"

The car door opens, and she sees Jarrod, Elizabeth's husband, get out and begin walking toward her. Her fear lessens but doesn't disappear; instead, it's joined by irritation.

"I'm okay, but please call me as soon as you know anything," Claire says.

"Remember to get in touch with Devon too, won't you," Mary-Rose says. "He'll help you if you need anything."

Claire ends the call with a quick, "Okay, bye."

Jarrod stops in front of Claire, looming over her. He folds his arms as he stands there, a smug smirk on his face. She knows this bullyboy tactic all too well: the silence is designed to unnerve her. So she stands her ground and waits.

"I'm glad I found you here." Jarrod grins. "I've come to apologize for my wife."

Claire frowns. "There's no need for that."

"Really?" Jarrod raises an eyebrow. "She told me she fired you."

Claire shrugs. "Well, perhaps I wasn't getting her the results she wanted."

Jarrod scoffs. "That's generous of you. Do you know how many trainers haven't managed to get her the results she wants? You kept her on track a lot longer than some of the others, and at least you had her using the bloody gym equipment properly. I can tell she likes you; she was just upset in the moment. Anyway, I want to offer you your job back. I've had a discussion with Elizabeth, and she can see she was being unreasonable. And I'd like you to train me too. For triple the money she was paying you before."

"You know what," Claire collects her bag and turns to leave, "I'm not sure how you even knew I was here, but I only train women. And if Elizabeth wants me back, Elizabeth can get in touch."

"It wasn't hard to find you." He looms over her, leering. "I checked the timetable online because I wanted to apologize in person—and I was hoping I'd make you an offer you couldn't refuse."

He couldn't have said anything more jarring. Each word resounds in Claire's mind, as she tries to hold his gaze and conceal how much he unnerves her. *He doesn't realize how clearly I see through him*, she thinks. *He's trying to appear chivalrous but flirty, and he probably thinks I'm already attracted to him.* His smile reminds her of a shark stealthily moving toward its target.

She goes to step around him. "Well, thank you. I'm sorry, but I'll have to go. Ask Elizabeth to call me, and we can talk."

Jarrod steps quickly to one side so he's in front of her again. "Hey," he says, reaching out and putting a hand on her arm, the heel of his palm brushing against her breast. "Don't be too hasty. I've heard you could do with the money."

Claire frowns. She can't remember telling Elizabeth about any money troubles. And the way Jarrod is ogling her makes her want to scream.

A long-ago voice leaps into her mind, with words that had been accompanied by another leer. *You look perfect to me. So, what do you reckon? I promise I won't bite. Or perhaps, if you're really lucky, I will.*

"Take your hand off me," she growls softly through gritted teeth.

Jarrod steps back, his expression changing, his smile morphing into a sneer. "Just remember," he says, following her as she hurries toward the front entrance, "I know a lot of people in this town. I could open plenty of doors for you. I understand your husband isn't working, and you're the breadwinner for the family. That's got to be tough." His attention moves to the building behind her. "Whatever they pay you here, I guarantee it's not as good as what's on offer in the mansions of Pep Grove and Mosman." He tucks a business card into the bag on her shoulder. "And if you're renting with Shipman and Fine, I might be able to swing you a rental reduction too if you talk to me nicely. Call me when you've had a chance to think about it."

She doesn't reply, hastening inside and moving to one of the corners behind the double doors, watching him strolling back to his car, one hand in his pocket. Whatever he wants, she has no intention of ever setting foot in his house again. She hadn't realized, until now, quite how much notice he was taking of her, but suddenly it's horribly clear. He's investigated her life. And he knows about Lenny. She thinks of those texts on Lenny's phone. Surely Jarrod isn't behind them? Or is this some kind of power play designed to interfere with her marriage and send her toward an affair? What does he know? And why choose her? There must be plenty of women around him that would say yes to a man like Jarrod. And yet this is happening to her. Again.

Her breath catches and she sits down quickly. There are voices in her head. *Bitch. Slag. Whore.*

There are so many strange things happening all at once that it's hard to think straight. She recalls her conversation with Mary-Rose.

Devon. He'll want to help.

She still has his number and texts him straightaway, her hand trembling as she types. *Do you remember what you taught me when you first met me, for protection? I think I might need it now. Can I meet you?*

She glances at the clock and sees it's almost time for her first private client of the day. She's sent out her SOS. Now the only thing to do is wait.

chapter eleven

LENNY

The playground is a ghost town as Lenny hurries toward the twins' classroom. He'd thought he might finally get some time on the guitar today, but after he'd persuaded Jake that Bob would be safe and he could go back to school, Mrs. Ainsley, the year-one teacher, had collared him saying she was short of parent help for the afternoon craft activity, and would he do her a huge favor . . . So Lenny had found himself agreeing to come back straight after lunch.

As he nears the classroom, his mobile rings. He pulls it from his pocket and sees it's Joanna. He hunches over against the chill of the wind as he stops to answer it.

"I've checked with the owners, and the lizard can stay," she says without preamble.

"That's good news," he replies, looking around at the deserted oval. It's strange seeing the school like this, when he's usually present during the chaos at the start and end of the day.

"Yes, but in return, that dent needs to be fixed pronto," she says, "or we're sending someone to do it and giving you the bill."

"All right," he sighs. "How long have I got?"

"Twenty-four hours."

He tries to smother a laugh. "Are you serious?"

"Lenny, you've had six months. I'm visiting your new neighbors tomorrow at lunchtime to go through some paperwork and I'd like to check it at the same time. It's almost an hour to get from the office to your house, and I don't want to have to come back again."

"Fine," he says, with as much good grace as he can muster. Really, what else is going to get thrown at him this week? It's only thirty-six hours until the gig, he thinks with a rush of nerves as he pockets his phone. Claire's right. Aside from the enforced DIY, he doesn't want to think about anything else until Saturday

For God's sake—it's one night in the local pub, not Wembley Stadium, he chides himself. The crowd at the local pub isn't going to hold him to account over a few missed chords or a stumbled word or two. But it's not the punters he's worried about, is it? It's Eddie's mate Baz and the casino gig, theirs for the taking if they get this right.

He shrugs off his worries and tentatively opens the door to the classroom, to see the kids are all sitting on the mat listening intently while Mrs. Ainsley shows them pictures of maths symbols and cartoon groups of animals on the whiteboard. Jake is at the front, his mouth hanging open in concentration, while on the opposite side of the group, Emily fiddles with a neon friendship bracelet on her wrist. Lenny tries to creep past them to the back room where the teachers prep the lessons, but Jake sees him and shouts, "Dad!" and Lenny watches Mrs.

Ainsley's shoulders drop as the kids all turn to look, and she loses everyone's attention in one fell swoop.

Lenny waves but then puts a finger to his lips and gestures with a twirling motion that they should turn back around. He hurries into the small room at the back to find the teacher's assistant is there cutting out colored squares of construction paper. Next to her is Saskia.

Saskia is obviously as surprised as Lenny. Her face goes bright red, and she turns back to her own task, putting different lengths of pipe cleaners into plastic tubs. The assistant, unawares, says, "Fantastic! More help! You're Jake and Emily's dad, yes?" and proceeds to instruct him on the under-the-sea craft activity they have planned for the next hour, and the different materials that will go into the tub for each table. Lenny tries to listen, but this isn't his forte, and as soon as she's gone, he turns to Saskia.

"Thanks for trying to help us this morning."

She smiles but her eyes stay focused on the table as she sorts through the craft detritus.

Lenny hesitates but can't help himself. "I lost a set of spare keys for a while too . . . You didn't find them, did you, and hang them up? They just suddenly reappeared."

Her gaze shoots up to meet his, and she frowns. "I don't know what you're talking about."

They stare at one another for a moment, and Lenny wishes he could read her better. He can't tell if Saskia's expression is one of confusion or discomfort. But when she doesn't say anything further, he begins to doubt himself, wondering why he's so suspicious of Saskia right now. Quickly, he looks for a way to break the tension.

"I hope you know what's going on here." He picks up some cotton buds and begins sorting them into different tubs.

"It's a children's craft," she says mock-admonishingly, a tease in her tone. "I reckon we can manage it."

They focus on the preparations, and Lenny begins taking the full bowls out to the tables, while Saskia finishes cutting strips of different shades of blue craft paper. On one of his return trips, she says, "You can trust me, Lenny, and you don't have to be awkward around me. I'm not going to force you into anything. You can take all the time you need."

She smiles at him and now he can sense both vulnerability and apprehension behind her words. This is more like the Saskia he knows—kind and considerate—and he realizes how unsettled he'd felt at being backed into a corner with no easy way out. It had made him doubt her, when perhaps he really should be more concerned about their strange new neighbor. Although he's not sure what either of the women would have to gain by taking Bob, except that it's thoroughly unnerved him.

As he catches Saskia's eye, she flushes and looks away, reminding him of the choice she's forced on him. They've gone quickly from clandestine kisses to her pushing him not just to acknowledge their affair but to make it official, and this isn't the relationship he'd thought he was in. The hand on his arm in full view of the school this morning had alarmed him—a claim on him that he isn't ready for. Perhaps she'd sensed that, and this is her way of backing off. But now she's put them in this position, he'll have to decide. It's either a full future with Saskia or the end of their time together. He tries to imagine the weeks ahead, without her easy laugh and playful nature, and finds the thought horribly depressing. But on his next trip into the classroom, Emily runs to him and grabs his leg and hugs it so hard that he has to hobble to the table. Jake asks him quietly if Bob is still okay, and he looks at the two of them and thinks of being responsible for splitting their family apart, taking them away from their mother, only seeing them for half the week. It's a wretched, wretched thought.

The next hour is lost in a whirlwind of helping children with craft glue and Popsicle sticks, with no privacy for intimate discussions, for which Lenny is extremely grateful. Saskia has already gone by the time Lenny leaves with Jake and Emily, each of his children proudly holding an underwater scene of coral and fish made out of a host of materials cut into triangles, circles, and squares. He places both artworks carefully onto the front seat of the car as he straps the kids into the back, and they talk enthusiastically about their day all the way home. As they enter the house, Jake heads straight to check on Bob, but Emily hears water running in the kitchen and shouts, "Mummy's home," grabbing her picture from Lenny and skipping through to the lounge.

Lenny follows and sees Claire taking Emily's proffered picture and admiring it. He waits until Emily has joined Jake in front of the TV, then asks, "How was your day?"

"Pretty standard," she says, going back to refilling her water bottle. "Yours?"

"I just spent the last hour cutting and pasting."

"Oh really?" She looks half-sympathetic and half-amused.

"Yeah, I'll have to try to rediscover my masculinity at band practice tonight," he adds as a joke but sees her face drop. "You'll be here, yes? You did remember?"

"I . . . I'd arranged to meet a new client," she says slowly, "but I'll figure it out. Do . . . do you think Lydia would mind coming over?"

Lenny tenses. "Well, she might do, since she had the kids yesterday evening, and she's having them tomorrow too."

"I'm really sorry, Lenny," Claire says, coming closer, keeping her voice low while glancing in the kids' direction. "I wouldn't ask if it weren't important."

He grimaces. Sighs. "I'll call her, but I can't guarantee it."

She touches his arm briefly. "Thank you. I need to take a quick shower, then I can look after the kids while you do whatever you need to."

He doesn't say anything, just watches her go. He thinks of Saskia and her consideration earlier and wonders why he's even fighting for this marriage.

He calls his mum, who says she'll be there in an hour, as they'd both known she would be. Whatever Lydia's plans are, she'll always drop them for the family, which is something Lenny tries hard not to take advantage of. As he thanks her and hangs up, he catches sight of Claire's phone on the countertop, hesitates, then picks it up, flicking the screen with his thumb but finding it locked. He's not sure of her code, so he sets it down, and looks across at the kids, to see Emily has turned away from the television to watch him.

"Are you trying to get into Mummy's phone?"

He feels himself redden. "I just needed to check something, and I can't be bothered to find mine . . ." As he talks, he can feel his phone burning a hole in his pocket.

Emily walks across. "I know her code," she says, tapping in *5791* and then going back over to Jake and their cartoon.

Lenny stares at the unlocked phone in front of him. He can hear the shower running. Quickly, he flicks onto calls, moving away from the kids into the hallway. There are plenty of numbers he doesn't recognize, so he takes out his phone and screenshots the first few. Then he moves to the texts. They're mostly to and from clients, but it's the one-third from the top that catches his eye. There's no name attached to the message, just the initials DN.

> Meet me at the City Beach lookout.
> Tonight. 7pm. D.

He's about to click on the message to see the entire thread when he hears the bedroom door open. He swipes out of the messages as he returns to the kitchen, hastily clicking the side button to relock the phone and laying it on the countertop.

His head rings with those insidious little words: *Your wife is a liar.* He puts the phone down, turning his grimace into a smile as he sees Emily watching him from the couch. But inside, he's furious. It looks like the anonymous troll is right. *What the hell are you doing, Claire?*

chapter twelve

CLAIRE

By the time Claire pulls into the parking lot, Devon is already waiting. She can see why he chose this spot: it's some distance from the beach, and there are only another couple of cars in the dozen or so spaces. The elevated position is perfect for watching the sun go down over the Indian Ocean, and Devon is sitting on the hood of his Hilux, eyes on the horizon as the last sliver of flaming orange sinks into the sea.

It's been over nine years since Claire's seen him, and he looks a fair bit older. His hair is still pulled back into a ponytail, but it's flecked with gray, and his deeply tanned face has more lines than it used to. But as she gets out of the car and he greets her with a wave, his expression is still the same: kind, world-weary, and stoic. He's wearing black jeans with an unbuttoned denim shirt over a Star Wars T-shirt with a picture of Grogu on it—a character that Claire can easily identify because Lenny, Jake, and Emily are all obsessed with *The Mandalorian*.

She walks quickly across. "I'm sorry to call you out of the blue."

He pats the hood. "I always said, didn't I? That's what I'm here for."

She climbs up to sit next to him. She's come in her work gear, after telling Lenny she was going to a client, and he looks her up and down. "Man, you're looking fit, Claire," he says approvingly. "I'm glad you kept up the training."

She smiles. "I train everyone else now, for a living," she says. "It seemed a good way to kill two birds with one stone."

"Well, sign me up. Let's face it, you were always my best student," he says with a chuckle. "And now the apprentice has become the master."

"I'll coach you if you give these up," she says, playfully flicking at the packet of cigarettes in his top pocket.

He chuckles. "Come on, we all need a vice."

She laughs. "Fair enough. I'd recommend coffee though. So how've you been?"

"Ah, all right. Got a dickey hip nowadays, but I'm still chasing around after Mum."

Claire has only met Devon's mum once, recalling an elderly lady with sallow, red-rimmed eyes whose hands had trembled when she'd taken Claire's and squeezed them.

"How is she?"

"She's pretty frail now—and she can't walk anymore. She's in a home; doesn't talk much when I visit."

They sit in silence for a moment, as the last light of the day turns the scattered stratus clouds pink and orange. "So," Devon says, watching the view, "you think he's found you?"

Claire stares at the darkening vista of empty sea and sky.

"Maybe. Perhaps I'm just being paranoid, but my husband has been getting texts every day for the last few weeks that say I'm a liar, goading him to ask me what the truth is. And we've got this strange woman who's moved in across the road who acts like she wants to be best friends and then casually mentioned Silverlakes yesterday—which is where he lived, and where . . . you know . . ." Her next quick inhale becomes a gulp that stalls her for a few seconds, then she adds, "I called Mary-Rose earlier, and she said she'd look into it for me—check he's still in prison—but I haven't heard back from her yet."

Devon doesn't move. "You know I'm not one to sugarcoat things. If your instincts are acting up, there's a reason. Trust them. We suffer when we don't."

She knows he's right, but it isn't what she wants to hear. She thinks again of the desolate expression on Devon's mother's face and the small grave that Claire had visited at Karrakatta Cemetery without telling anyone. Devon's sister Misha had been gone for almost twenty years by the time Claire met Devon, and yet Claire felt a kinship with her that was beyond words. Devon had never spoken directly to Claire about what had happened, but Mary-Rose had told her the story. Misha was one of the women who featured in Claire's nightmares, as they ran together from vengeful monsters, until backed into corners from which there would be no escape.

"Are you still doing the training?" she asks him.

"Won't stop until I die," he answers. His eyes move back toward the ocean for a moment, but she senses there's something on his mind. She waits, and eventually, he says, "Did you ever get in touch with anyone from home, Claire?"

"No," she says instantly. "I haven't spoken to anyone."

"You've not sent anything back—a gift, or a message through a friend—nothing?"

She's about to say no. Then stops.

Lenny shifts position to look at her. "What is it?"

"Years ago, when Lenny and I got married in Vegas, I sent a picture to my sister. From America. The photo was of the back of us, holding hands under a Vegas sign. You couldn't see my face, or Lenny's. And my hair—it was a different color. It was one of those instant prints, and I just . . ."

She pauses. Devon doesn't move or speak, but Claire is riven with guilt.

"I'm sorry, perhaps it was foolish. But that was ten years ago. Surely it can't be relevant now? I promise I thought the whole thing through, and I was sure it couldn't be traced. I just—" her voice cracks, "I wanted her to know I was okay. I haven't sent anything else, before or since."

She wishes Devon would tell her that this is okay but knows he won't. He takes in what she's told him and then says, "All right then. Well, let me have a think about that. Can you send me a picture of the photo you're talking about?"

"Sure."

"Okay. Meanwhile, I brought ya something." He jumps off the hood and moves to the car while she waits, reappearing in front of her with a reusable zipped-up shopping bag. FRESH FOODS is emblazoned on the side. He hands it to her, and it's heavier than she expects.

"Keep it in there, but you can take a look," he encourages her.

She unzips the bag and peers into it, to see there's an object wrapped in some kind of small tablecloth with flowers on it. She pulls back the wrapping a little, and the dark metal of the gun glints beneath one of the overhead lights of the parking lot. It's icy cold beneath her fingers.

"It's a Beretta. Loaded, with the safety on. Do you still remember how to use it?" he asks.

She nods, remembering how he'd trained her, back when she first arrived. The multiple trips to the shooting range as he patiently ensured she could hit a target.

"I think so, yes."

"Good." He gestures toward the bag. "It's untraceable, so don't worry about that, but keep it safe."

She stares at the bag, suddenly feeling the absurdity of the situation. What's she really going to do with this?

Devon is watching her intently. His warm, calloused hand reaches out to pat hers. "Don't overthink it," he cautions. "You won't use it unless you have to. But it's insurance. What did I always tell you?"

"If no one is coming to save me," she says quietly. "I need to save myself."

"Absolutely," he says. "And now you have a family to think of too. How are those little ones?"

"As human beings? They're amazing. As two little lives I'm responsible for? Utterly exhausting."

He chuckles and puts an arm around her, giving her back a quick pat. As they sit there watching the sky darken, Claire realizes she hasn't felt as safe as this in a long time. She'd forgotten how good it is to be with someone who knows the truth of her life and is still on her side. All those years ago, when she'd arrived in Perth, Devon had been the only one she could turn to, and he'd made it his mission to give her strength in every way he could. But he hadn't just taught her self-defense and how to shoot—he'd also made her laugh, taken the mickey out of her, and tried to lighten her up. "You can't carry your kind of burden for every hour of every day," he'd once told her. "The weight of it will get too much if you do. If you want to stay healthy, and stay alive, you have to get practiced at setting your baggage down for a while and not picking it up too often."

Claire's not sure how she's fared on that score. She's a functional human being, yes, going through the motions of each day. But a fulfilled one? That goal is a lot more elusive.

Devon jumps off the hood and holds out a hand to help her climb down. "We should go. Get that stowed somewhere safe." He nods at the bag. "You know you can call anytime, if you need me."

"I know," she says. "Thank you."

He waits, watching, as she gets in her car and drives away.

chapter thirteen

LENNY

Lenny is lying behind a sand dune as the last of the daylight disappears. He's been watching his wife sitting on the hood of a Hilux with a man who looks like a cross between a bouncer and a wiry old rocker. Only last night, Lenny had agreed with Claire that he needed to focus on the gig, and yet here he is, against his better nature, beginning to shiver on the wet sand, instead of heading to the penultimate rehearsal with the band.

To add to his annoyance, Claire appears way more relaxed than he's seen her in a long time. Lenny had watched as the man passed her some kind of insulated food bag, and after she'd peered inside, they'd hugged. He tries to imagine what might be in there; he'd guess it isn't frozen food. Whatever it is, he hates it, because it's part of the reason he has found himself crouching in the dunes like a peeping tom, wondering how the hell this can be his life.

As Claire drives away, he checks his watch, knowing he's cutting it close to get to the practice on time. But there hadn't been a choice, because there's no way he would be able to focus and lose himself in the music while his wife had some kind of secret rendezvous. He'd half-expected to find himself watching a romantic affair, and had anticipated heartbreak if that's what it was, because Claire had intimated that the open marriage was all about his needs, not hers, and he wanted to believe her. However, this is different, and in some ways worse. It hadn't seemed romantic, but there was an intimacy between the man and Claire that is making Lenny seethe with jealousy. What had this guy done that Claire could turn to him, when she's refused to let Lenny into her emotional space for so long?

His mother had seemed worried tonight as he'd left the house. "You look exhausted, Lenny," Lydia had said. "Are you nervous about tomorrow?"

He'd wanted to explain to her that he'd struggled to focus on the gig over the past few days, which, in truth, did twist his stomach a little because he wants to be on top of his game, and he's anything but. He's begun having horrific mental flashes of himself singing listlessly and off-key, while the band plays on miserably and half the school community stares glumly into their drinks.

He'd avoided mentioning any of this, instead saying, "I'm okay," and apologizing to his mum for the extra babysitting. "You'll end up having the kids every night this week."

She'd waved him away. "They're my grandkids, they're not a chore, you know. And Claire asked me herself about tomorrow," she'd said, her eyes shining. "I'm so glad she wants to go and support you rather than stay here. And while I'd love to hear you sing, I'm never going to say no to helping your marriage stay strong. One day I'll crack her shell, and we'll be best friends," she'd added, giving Lenny a kiss on the cheek.

He'd appreciated the optimism but could only imagine his mother's stunned expression if she could see what they were both up to this evening.

Lenny waits for a moment, watching the man's car begin to move, and then slowly gets to his feet. He turns away and hurries south, heading back to his own car in the next parking lot, checking the time, and seeing he'll have to drive fast if he's going to make it by eight. The uneven sand slows his pace, and he's breathing loud enough not to hear the footsteps until they're almost upon him.

A crushing weight lands heavily on his shoulders, his knees are taken out from under him, and he falls to the ground with a thud, trying to fight back, his assailant rolling him over to look into his face.

It's the man from the Hilux, and he looks furious.

"I saw you lying in the sand dunes, spying," the man barks. "Who the hell are you, and what do you want?"

He tugs on the top of Lenny's T-shirt, pulling him up so they eyeball one another. From here it's clear they're no physical match. The man is solid, trained muscle. Lenny's heart is pounding, but one defiant part of him boils with rage.

"Claire's my wife," he yells into the man's face. "So perhaps *you* can explain to *me* what the fuck you two were doing up there?"

The man shoves him away roughly and stares at him. Lenny can see his mind working, trying to get a handle on this information while Lenny glares back in confusion, on his knees in the sand. It's as though the man had thought he was someone else.

"I'm sorry, mate," he says at last, as Lenny's breathing begins to return to normal. "You must be Lenny."

Lenny's head spins. "What the hell is going on?"

The man sits down in the sand next to him. "Again, I'm sorry, buddy, but that's a conversation you need to have with your wife."

"You're not . . . you're not having an affair, are you?" Lenny stutters, knowing it doesn't feel right but unable to come up with anything else to ask.

At this, the man begins to laugh. It starts as a throaty chuckle but then becomes a rasp that racks his entire body, doubling him over as it turns into a smoker's cough.

"Have you taken a good look at me?" the man wheezes as he recovers and sits next to Lenny on the sand. "I'll think you'll find I'm twenty years too old and not really Claire's type." Lenny says nothing, still failing to see what's so funny. The man catches sight of Lenny's unamused expression and stops laughing. "Seriously, I'm just a friend, mate," he says. He looks intently at Lenny. "She says you're one of the good guys."

"Does she now?" Lenny raises his eyebrows. "That's interesting, because I'm not sure she wants to confide in me anymore."

The man takes his time before replying. "I'm sorry she hasn't told you her whole story, but she has her reasons." He considers Lenny for a long moment, and Lenny can see the debate raging in his eyes. He watches Devon run one hand over his face and across his wispy gray beard, before he sighs, holding Lenny's gaze intently, as he adds, "There are horrors in her past: things she'll find difficult to ever say out loud. Deep down, she's been frightened for a long time now—more frightened than you or I could ever imagine. So while it's not my place to share her secrets, please let me offer you some advice. Hang in there. Trust her, okay?" He stands up and brushes the sand off his jeans, before adding, "From what she told me tonight, she might be in danger. And if she is, then so are you."

chapter fourteen

CLAIRE

Claire sits in the corner of the bar, back to the wall. She's never been here before, but that's the point: she needs a place to hide for a while. It's quiet except for a couple of middle-aged men playing pool and a few old-timers sitting on barstools staring at the TV in the corner. No one has taken any notice of her as she skulks in a booth in the shadows.

One drink, she'd said to herself, and then she'd go home. But she'd finished that almost two hours ago, and had ordered a soft drink instead, and then, after she judged enough time had passed, she'd downed another Jack Daniel's and Coke.

She can't stop picturing that shopping bag in her car. She'd wanted this, but now it's making her feel like a different person. Paranoid. Dangerous.

Alone.

She hates that Ryan can do this to her, even now, after all this time. That she can still see his face so clearly: the need and desperation on that last awful night together, when he'd forced her into his car, headlights flashing wildly in the darkness as he'd driven out of town, and she'd thought it would be her last night on earth.

Sometimes she tries to pinpoint the moment when she realized he was a monster. In the beginning she'd been entirely fooled: when he'd begun turning up at the gym at the same time as she trained, she'd been flattered, and had enjoyed training alongside him. He was attentive, showing her how she might lift a little more weight, or push a little bit harder on the treadmill and rowing machines. He'd been impressed that she'd taken a whole year out to focus on her athletics training; and that she was tipped for a run at the Commonwealth Games long-jump team. He'd built up her ego alongside his own, and to begin with it was just a bit of fun.

Until it wasn't.

Claire downs her drink, irritated at being so maudlin. What has she got to feel sad or resentful about really, when she's had another chance at life? And what has she done with this gift? Because while she's tried her best not to live in fear, she can't help but push people away. She's practically encouraged Lenny into Saskia's arms. She shuts down the conversation every time Lydia tries to talk to her. She keeps herself so busy with work that she's got no time for friends. She can't even get in touch with the family she loves and left behind. And as for the kids: well, she's gotten pretty good at suspending her anxiety for small amounts of time so she can provide the kind of entertainment and attention they need, as long as someone else is close by. Alone with them it's a lot harder; less safe somehow. They sap her energy, leaving nothing for the kind of emotional and physical intimacy Lenny has long been hoping for. And she's always been too scared of another unexpected pregnancy, and the associated emotions that come with it, to let him anywhere near her physically.

And yet Saskia's claim on him is gnawing away at her. She'd tried to pretend that the physical side of things didn't matter; that it was good if someone else could give Lenny things she isn't capable of right now. But she doesn't want him to leave. She's put them in this holding pattern, thinking that somehow, one day, they would escape it, but without any idea of how. What else could she have possibly expected? That he would stay forever? How can she even think about that if she can't give him the relationship he so clearly craves?

She swigs her drink as different plans and possibilities tumble through her mind. If she just walked away, she would take the danger of Ryan with her. Lenny would no doubt turn to Saskia, who would welcome them all with open arms, love and mother the kids, and eventually, they would forget all about Claire. And she would be free: without the weight of anyone's crushing need for her. Without the guilt of offering only a half life in return, constructed on lies.

But then she remembers Emily's face at the assembly, how it had blossomed at just the sight of Claire. And not only that, but the way Claire's heart had felt in return: jolted by a magnetic pull so forceful that it took extra concentration not to move closer to her daughter. How could she deny that? How could she pretend that Emily would forget her, when Claire hasn't seen her mother or Candace or Robbie in over eleven years, and yet she thinks about them every single day?

The night is full of impossible choices, and she's light-headed by the time her phone buzzes in her pocket. She takes it out, expecting it to be Lydia politely inquiring when she'll be back, or Lenny growling at her because she isn't home. Or even Elizabeth, who has texted twice already, asking if they can talk, probably pushed on by Jarrod. But it's none of them: it's Mary-Rose. She checks her watch. It's eight thirty. Which means it's after midnight in New Zealand. This must be important.

She answers the call with cold dread settling into her bones.

"Hello, my dear." There's a portentous note to Mary-Rose's usually assured calmness that immediately makes Claire's breath stall. "I'm sorry to call so late, but I've done some research for you, and there are a few things you need to know."

"All right," Claire replies quickly, her thoughts still lingering on her loved ones, her chest on fire with nerves.

Mary-Rose's tone is gentle. "Let me tell you about your family first. They're all okay."

Claire allows herself a gulp of air. "Thank god," she whispers.

"Have you looked them up at all in the past eleven years?"

"I . . . I haven't dared. I couldn't bear to. It would have made the pull so strong, and I knew I had to stay away from them, to keep them safe," she explains, even though she knows Mary-Rose already understands all this, that together they've already been through the choices she made and why. "I . . . I told Devon earlier that I sent my sister a photo, ten years ago, after I got married. It was of Lenny and me with our backs to the camera. I really hope that hasn't triggered anything, but I was so careful, and I can't see how. Please, tell me about them?"

"They're doing well, sweetheart. Your mum is still busy with the gift shop. And your sister . . . she's married and has a gorgeous baby boy. Your brother joined the army for a while, and now he's set up his own recording studio in Auckland. They all seem to be thriving from what I can see."

Claire is glad she's sitting in the corner of the bar, turned away from the rest of the customers, so they can't see the tears streaming down her face.

"Oh, okay. And what about Tilly and Gary, did you find anything I should be worried about?"

"No. I found out their rental agent is the same as yours— Shipman and Fine—and I've left a message there to see if I can get some more information, perhaps look at references. I'll continue to investigate and see how I go. But if they were in Silverlakes, so far I can't find a record of them there."

"All right. Thank you." Claire waits, but Mary-Rose doesn't say any more, and Claire is suddenly aware of the tension in the silence between them.

"Is there anything else?" she asks cautiously.

"There is something. Are you sitting down, dear?"

Mary-Rose's tone is ominous and the skin on Claire's neck prickles. She readies herself.

"It seems that Ryan has been temporarily moved from Pare-moremo—and no one wants to talk about where he's gone."

The room suddenly feels far away from her and when Claire opens her eyes again, she wonders if she'd blacked out for a moment, as Mary-Rose is speaking again. "Claire? Are you still there?"

"So no one knows where he is?" she whispers into the phone.

"Well, someone must, but lips are sealed. And I'm still looking into it," Mary-Rose says, "but because the information is classified, I need to find the right person who's willing to share."

Claire's fingers are tingling, and she realizes she's squeezing the phone so tightly that she's cutting off her circulation. She holds the phone between her shoulder and ear, massaging her wrist, trying to slow her breathing and calm her pounding heart. She'd been expecting this, she realizes. Somehow, Ryan has been released from prison and of course no one will have told her, because no one knows where she is or even that she's alive. Why hadn't she made more of an effort to keep track of him? Why has she let him come back to haunt her and catch her unawares? Even though she'd decided to leave everyone behind, she could still have watched from afar. She could have been her family's guardian angel, rather than turning her back on them all. But it had just been too painful to witness them getting on with their lives.

"So he could be anywhere?" she says shakily.

"I don't think so," Mary-Rose says, with a surprising degree of confidence, Claire thinks. "There's a long official process for releasing prisoners, and none of that has happened. He's just . . . missing. I'm still trying to figure out what to make of it, but the important thing right now is not to panic. Sit tight, and I'll call you as soon as I know more."

chapter fifteen

LENNY

By the time Lenny heads into the back room of the swanky Oceanside Bar, clutching his guitar case, his head is pounding. There's palpable tension in the room as his three bandmates turn from their discussion to stare at him, but no one says a word. He wants to explain, to say to them: *I just met a man on the beach who told me that Claire and I might be in danger, and then he disappeared into the night. What the hell do you think that means?* Instead, he says, "Sorry I'm late," hoping to dispel the awkward silence.

Everyone glances at one another, but no one speaks.

"What's going on?" Lenny asks, setting his case down and taking off his jacket, wondering if they can really be this pissed off with him for being twenty minutes late.

"Dave wants to change the set," Eddie says with a tone of disgust. Fletcher pulls a face at Lenny, which shows his disapproval, but for whom Lenny isn't sure. Lenny has known

Fletcher and Dave since school, but Eddie had been a late-comer to the band after their original guitarist had moved to Thailand to study Buddhism, and he'd never quite gelled with the rest of them.

"Don't you think people have moved on a bit from Cold-play and Maroon 5?" Dave interjects. "I'm not saying we shouldn't do any of the old stuff, but we could add in some more contemporary songs."

"What were you thinking?" Lenny asks.

"I reckon we could do a really good version of Pink's 'Walk Me Home,' or what about Avicii's 'Hey Brother'?"

"You know he died." Eddie rolls his eyes. "And that song's almost a decade old?"

"Oh, fuck off, Eddie," Dave replies. "That song's awesome, and I'm just trying to jazz up our middle-aged musos vibe—make sure Baz doesn't think we're twenty years out of date."

Eddie grimaces. "It's too late. We're performing on Friday, and Jillian wants me to get on with the rehearsal tonight so I can help her with the bloody cookies for the kids' bake sale tomorrow. She's sick of me going out so much, so can we just do what we rehearsed?"

Lenny catches Fletcher's eye, who shrugs and goes to sit behind the drum kit, waiting. They all look at Lenny.

"I kinda like Dave's idea," he says, as Eddie begins shaking his head furiously. "Hang on a minute, mate, hear me out. We know our old stuff inside out. What if we just practice a few new songs tonight—no pressure—and if we like them, we'll add them in, and if we don't, then we haven't really lost anything."

"Thank you!" Dave says triumphantly, gesturing toward Lenny appreciatively.

Eddie mutters away as they go about setting up, but an hour later, even he is smiling as Lenny holds the last note of "Riptide" and Dave finishes the guitar accompaniment with a flourish.

"Say I'm wrong now," Dave says triumphantly.

Before anyone can answer, Pete the landlord, tall, stocky, and completely bald, opens the door. "Sounding good fellas. Wanna take a break? I'll shout each of you a pint."

"Sounds good to me," Dave says, standing his guitar carefully against the wall. Eddie and Lenny follow suit and they traipse out into the main bar, finding a table in the corner.

"Aren't you on cookie duty?" Fletcher grins at Eddie.

"Screw you." Eddie chucks a bar mat at him. "At least I'm only called upon occasionally, unlike Mr. Househusband here." He gestures at Lenny, who refuses to take the bait. They all profess to be new age men but they can't resist having a dig at him now and again for the full-time dad role, which they obviously see as the ultimate emasculation. Lenny doesn't give a shit, having never felt a particular affinity with traditional ideas of masculinity to begin with, probably thanks to his parents. His father, Leo, had carved wooden sculptures for a living before he died from cancer in Lenny's teens, and his mother had always encouraged him to be emotionally open and empathetic and to steer clear of toxic groups of men who enjoyed competing for dominance.

"You know, there's a rumor going around school about you and Saskia Adams," Eddie says suddenly.

Lenny puts down his pint with a bump. "What?"

They all gape at him. Fletcher's mouth falls open. "Seriously? You're cheating on Claire?"

101

"I'm not fucking cheating on Claire," Lenny says, his face reddening. "We've . . . we've got an open marriage."

He's reduced the men to complete silence, and it stays like this for at least thirty seconds, until Eddie snorts. "How the hell did you manage that?"

Lenny glances around at them all. Fletcher appears intrigued, while Dave seems worried. And Eddie, who is the only one who has kids at the same school and might know Saskia, looks amused.

Instead of answering the question, Lenny asks Eddie, "What exactly have you been told?"

"Lara said she heard it from a group of mums."

"Oh shit. So it's all around the school then?"

"Quite likely, mate. And Lara thinks you're playing with fire—says the ex-husband is mental and Saskia can be . . . well, 'dramatic' was the word she used."

Lenny takes a long sip of beer and closes his eyes. There're only a few ways this could have happened. Either someone has seen him and Saskia together—not likely, since they were careful and never went out and about as a couple—or Saskia has told people. Which wasn't the agreement. Lenny didn't care about the school parents' gossip, but he minded very much if someone let something slip to a child, and the rumor fell into the ears of Emily or Jake. And he doesn't want Claire to be the subject of speculation and pitying glances either.

His bandmates sense his discomfort and go easy on him, turning the conversation back to deciding which songs they still need to practice, and what's likely to make the final performance. They go back into rehearsal after the drinks, and everyone works hard on all the small details they're wanting to nail down before tomorrow. It's almost eleven by the time they say their goodbyes.

As Lenny heads out into the half-empty parking lot, he hears his name being called. Dave is running to catch up with him. "You okay, mate?" Dave asks, clapping Lenny on the back.

Lenny straightens. "Honestly? I don't know."

"You surprised me in there." Dave gestures back to the pub. "I've always thought you and Claire were a great match. And don't take this the wrong way," he gives Lenny a rueful grin, "but I've never thought of you as an open-marriage kind of guy."

Despondent, Lenny nods. "I'm not, really. It's just, things have been weird since the kids were born. Claire thought it might be better . . ."

"Ah," Dave says.

Lenny is immediately indignant. "What?"

"Just like I said, you're not an open-marriage kind of guy. Neither am I—jeez, I can't imagine what I'd do if Sandra wanted . . ." He tails off. "Sorry," he adds, "but I've known you since you were thirteen. I just thought it must have come from Claire."

"She isn't sleeping with anyone else," Lenny retorts defensively. "At least not as far as I know. She . . . this was her idea, but it was because she couldn't . . . didn't want to have sex. Because she was struggling so much after the twins were born."

Dave's mouth drops open. He doesn't have to say anything, because Lenny is seeing his life through Dave's eyes. Claire had struggled after the children. She'd pushed Lenny away and given him an easy way out. And Christ, he'd taken it. What the hell had he been thinking? Why hadn't he fought harder for his family? For his wife?

Lenny says a hasty goodbye to Dave and drives home on the edge of the speed limit, desperate to get back to Claire. But instead of his wife waiting for him, he finds his mother sitting on the floor with Jake in his pajamas, playing Hungry Hungry Hippos.

"I'm really sorry," Lydia says ruefully as Jake grabs onto Lenny's legs in a bear hug, "but he couldn't sleep, and he was quite distressed until we started this."

Lenny thinks of the school run tomorrow and sighs. "Come on, buddy, let's get you to bed," he says, picking Jake up and carrying him to his room. He sits with him for a few minutes until the boy is asleep, and when he returns to the lounge, his mum is already wearing her coat, her bag in hand. "I'm sorry, Lenny," she says again, "he was crying and he wouldn't go back to bed for me. I didn't know what else to do."

"It's okay." Lenny kisses Lydia on the forehead. "Thank you. Where's Claire? Have you heard from her?"

Lydia puts a hand on his arm. "No," she says. "But your neighbor turned up holding these, said she found them on the doorstep."

He turns and sees a huge bouquet of roses sitting on the kitchen counter, cut and arranged in a clear vase with a ruby-red ribbon wrapped around it. He goes across and picks up the card attached to one of the stems.

"For Claire, it seems," Lydia adds, her tone cautious. "I presume they're not from you then?"

Lenny reads the card. *From your secret admirer.*

He puts it down, his jaw clenched hard. "No. Not from me."

"I don't know what's going on with you both," Lydia says, coming over to kiss him on the cheek. "But you need to talk. For the little ones' sake as well as yours."

"I know, Mum," he says, checking his watch. It's gone eleven. *Where the hell is Claire?*

Lydia turns to leave. "Your new neighbor seems nice, anyway," she adds, heading for the door.

He frowns. "You said she was holding these?"

She turns back, surprised at his tone. "Yes—said she found them on the front doorstep. She wanted to borrow some teabags."

Lenny instinctively walks over to Bob's cage, checking the lizard is still there. "I don't want you inviting her in, okay? She's . . . weird."

Lydia shrugs. "Really? I thought that Bob's disappearance was a mix-up in the end? And she seemed fine to me. Very chatty and friendly." She comes closer to Lenny. "Are you okay, love? You've got dark circles under your eyes. Are you not sleeping?"

"I'm fine, Mum, there's just a lot going on this week."

Lydia shrugs and rubs her eyes. "Okay, well I need to get home to bed. Call me if you need anything," she says as she heads for the door.

Lenny checks the kids are asleep, grateful that Jake has turned to the wall and is breathing deeply. Back in the lounge, he begins to pace back and forth, unable to do more than look at the clock, and the message on the card. He thinks about going to bed, but there's no way he'll sleep. He texts Claire.

Where are you?

It's after midnight when the front door finally opens, and Claire creeps in quietly. Lenny marches up to her, causing her to jump as he hisses, "Where have you been?"

"Christ, Lenny, you frightened me," she says. "I thought you'd be asleep by now. What's wrong?"

"Oh, I don't know—how about the fact that my wife doesn't give a shit about this family and lets my mum do her half of the childcare. Or that I saw you and some guy sitting on a Hilux watching the sunset together tonight? Or that the same guy jumped me and told me I might be in danger? Or that everyone in the bloody school thinks I'm a bastard for having an affair with Saskia. Or that you have a secret admirer." He brandishes the flowers at her. "I mean, apart from all that, I'm feeling fucking fine."

Claire takes the flowers from him and reads the card. He waits, watching her.

She puts them down and goes to sit on the sofa, and when she looks up at him, he's shocked to see her eyes are filled with tears. Claire never cries.

She wipes her face. "I . . . I thought it might be over," she says. "But that," she gestures to the flowers, "tells me it's not. And I have no idea what's going on."

Lenny sits down next to her. "Claire, I'm sorry, this is all so messed up. But I'm here, okay? I want to help. Please just explain what you can. The guy on the beach tonight—he scared me. Whatever is happening, I need to know."

Claire looks at him. "Promise me you'll just listen," she says.

"I promise." *This is it*, he realizes. *She's finally going to talk.* His heart begins to race.

"Okay then. First of all," she says, with a deep breath, "my name hasn't always been Claire."

Lenny stares at her, incredulous. "What are you talking about?"

106

Claire can hardly bear to look at her husband, painfully aware of the mixture of confusion and betrayal in his eyes. "I've been Claire Wilson for the past eleven years," she explains, "but I used to be called Lucy Rutherford. Something happened to me when I was nineteen, a year before I met you, and I had to leave everyone I loved behind." She hesitates. Lenny's mouth has fallen open, and his eyes are wide, but it's too late to stop now. "Look," she says, suddenly aware of their children asleep in the adjacent rooms, "let me try to explain from the beginning."

chapter sixteen

CLAIRE

It's painful to allow the memories in when she's been holding them back for so long. Alone, she can try to pretend that Ryan is the only one who stalks her nightmares . . . but, there's another person who haunts her: and she doesn't know how she'll even bear to say his name, let alone tell Lenny the whole story.

She reaches back far enough into the past to find a safe place to start and takes a deep breath. "When I was eighteen, I took a year off from studying because I had a shot at reaching the national athletics team," she begins. "I was rated in the top twenty-five across the country at long-jump, and among the top fifty sprinters too."

"O-kay," Lenny says, sitting back in confusion. "That's a sizable chunk of new information about you."

She balks at his tone. "There's a lot more to come, so if you want me to tell you about this, you'll need to let me finish without interrupting," she says testily.

He doesn't reply but holds up his hands in contrition.

"I was going hard on the training," Claire continues, "and I started strength sessions at the local gym. I'd been there about a month when I began bumping into this guy called Ryan." She works hard to keep her voice even, as it begins to slip and crack on the name. "He was very friendly, obviously interested in me, and he began turning up when he knew I'd be there, helping me with different equipment. And I didn't stop him," she says. "I just thought he was kind and helpful."

It's unnerving to remember how she'd felt at the time. She'd completely misread his swagger as confidence, and his attention as normal attraction. Therefore, in hindsight she felt she'd unwittingly encouraged him for way too long. He'd given her lots of advice about using the gym equipment properly, which meant he'd often touched her: gently pushing her legs in the right position for maximum extensions or pushing the heel of his hand against her shoulders as she worked on the chest press. At the time she hadn't minded: their chemistry was instant, and she was grateful that the exercise accounted for the flush that regularly stole across her face. But now it's one of the hardest things to remember: how completely she'd been fooled.

"Eventually, he asked me out . . ." She hesitates, recalling those first inklings of something amiss. Ryan had turned up with a bunch of twelve long-stemmed roses, but then hadn't talked to her at all during the car ride, singing along to thrash metal instead and drumming on the steering wheel, his head jerking around in time with the music. She'd sat awkwardly, not wanting to join in, and it had been a long forty-five minutes to get to Takapuna. At a little beach-shack restaurant they were shown to a table outside with a view of the water. Ryan obviously knew the chef, who had told her to order anything she wanted from the menu, on the house. She'd focused on the list of food, while, opposite her, Ryan picked up a toothpick and twirled it idly against parted lips. The way he'd studied her with such open desire had made her nervous and not particularly hungry, so she'd ordered a salad, and as they ate he'd told her about his work as a bouncer for one of the clubs in Auckland—Cloud Nine—and she'd nodded along even though she'd never heard of it. When he'd left to talk at some length with the manager, she'd waited uncomfortably, playing on her phone and reassuring her mum, who was messaging, concerned about where she was. When a waitress, who'd brought her some water, had whispered, "Be careful," as she'd set down the glass, Claire had looked sharply at the woman—young and pretty, with long dark hair and almond-shaped eyes—unsure if she'd misheard. But the woman had held her gaze for a moment before moving away.

Lenny is waiting as Claire succumbs to the memories, and she realizes she's stopped talking. "On that first evening alone together, I realized how uncomfortable I actually felt around him," she tells him. "Away from the gym, it was clear we didn't have much in common. He was obsessed with looks and designer labels, and when he introduced me to people it was as his hot future-Olympian girlfriend. I quickly realized that dating me was essentially about bragging rights."

Lenny is listening intently, leaning forward, his eyes not leaving hers. But there's so much detail that Claire can't possibly explain everything. Her mind flashes backward again, to the walk on the beach after that one and only dinner, when Ryan had suddenly picked her up and threatened to run into the sea with her, and she'd squealed and laughed along, knowing that's what he wanted—even though it hadn't felt good anymore. She'd only felt safe because there were plenty of people around as the sun drifted stealthily toward the horizon. When he'd put her down, he'd taken hold of her hand, and they'd stayed like that until they reached a group of trees, where he'd pulled her into the shadows beneath the branches, out of sight of the other beachgoers. He'd walked her back until she was leaning against one of the thick trunks, put his hands on her waist, gazed into her eyes, and kissed her with force, pressing his lips hard onto hers, crushing her with his tight, sculpted body. There had been a raw urgency and intensity to him that was terrifying, his stubble scratching her mouth as the cold, rough tree bark rubbed hard against her back. As soon as she could breathe, she'd said, "I need to go home now," and he'd pulled back and looked at her, his body still pinning her against the tree, showing her who was really in charge. But then he'd given her one of those wide, brilliant smiles, and stepped away, holding out his hand. "Of course," he'd said—but only after the long car journey back to Tetherton, once she was safely at home again, had her breathing ceased catching in her throat and slowly returned to normal.

Opposite her, Lenny waits for more, his narrow face pale and his soft gray eyes confused. She tries to imagine what it's like for him, hearing this sudden and unexpected story about the woman he's lived with and loved for a decade. And although she's long dreaded this moment, it's a relief to lay it out in front of him. He still has no idea what's coming, but Pandora's box is well and truly open, and there's nothing for it except to continue talking.

"I switched gyms after that night," she says. "I went to

one called Horizons that was a lot more expensive, but which felt safer. I really hoped that would be the last I would see of Ryan—and for a few months, it was. I loved it at the new place because some of the other athletics club members went there too, including this lovely, gentle guy called Todd," she adds, choking up as she remembers. She wants to say, *He was so much like you*—but it isn't the time. She's always seen the similarities between Todd and Lenny: the music, the gentleness, and their withdrawal whenever they felt threatened or uncomfortable. But she doesn't want Lenny to wonder if that's why she chose him, once he's heard the whole story.

"I recognized Todd from stadium training but I hadn't really spoken to him much before. He was quiet and earnest, but he was also one of the club's rising stars: tipped for long-distance finals in the next Olympics. We began spending more and more time together, and I really liked him."

The next flash of memory comes with a pang of heart-break: the first proper conversation between her and Todd. "I've never thought of long-distance runners needing so many gym sessions," she'd joked to him one Thursday afternoon when he'd come out of the weights room looking particularly sweaty.

"You mean because we're puny?" he'd laughed.

But he hadn't been puny. His body was all hardwired muscle, his face lean, and his dark brown eyes full of promise. When she began working at a bakery to help meet her training costs, he'd waited for her at the end of shifts, and they'd gone home to cook dinner together, hanging out in her room watching TV on nights off from training. Often, he'd bring his guitar and practice softly while she read; it was his other passion aside from running. Their friends at the athletics club all acted as if their sudden pairing was the most natural thing in the world, and one night, as she and half a dozen mates were creased up with laughter at one of Todd's jokes, she had realized what the others had already seen: they were a natural, happy fit—bringing out the best in one another. Todd made her feel comfortable and safe; he knew how to laugh at himself, and to gently poke fun at her so she wouldn't take life too seriously.

"Claire?"

She doesn't realize there are tears on her cheeks until Lenny's voice intrudes into her thoughts, and she quickly wipes them away. "Sorry. It's hard thinking about it all. Anyway, Todd and I had a really good couple of months, and by the time Ryan reappeared and started coming into Horizons, we were inseparable. Ryan didn't like that at all. He never approached us, but he'd be there at the gym, doing his own workout alongside ours, and I could feel him watching us. All the anxiety I'd felt at the old place returned, and I began missing sessions, checking out the parking lot before I went in, trying to go at unusual times or at least always when Todd was there, so I felt safer. Of course, this played havoc with my training schedule, and it continued for weeks with Ryan just watching us, doing nothing." She takes a big breath. "Until one day he drove slowly behind us all the way home after a training session. Todd and I were both unnerved by it, unsure what to do about such obvious stalking. Close to my house, Ryan suddenly kicked his ute into gear and roared away—and I had to explain to Todd what had happened before, and who this guy was. I said I thought Ryan was sending me a message, and Todd laughed at first and said, 'What's the message? That he's intending to stalk you?' But when he saw my expression, he sobered up fast and looked as frightened as I felt.

"The next day, Ryan came back into Horizons and immediately challenged Todd to a bench-pressing competition, hustling up to him in the gym like he wanted to start a fight—and Todd said no, laughing it off, and Ryan said something scathing about his physique not being up to it, trying to goad him. Todd looked confused, but he was clearly uncomfortable, and we left quickly. However, a few days later, I decided to go to the gym alone, and Ryan turned up and followed me around, telling me my boyfriend was a prick who obviously couldn't handle the competition. Eventually, the manager realized what was happening and chucked Ryan out, but I was really shaken and I had to call my sister to pick me up. When I told her about it, she thought we should go to the police, but I was worried it might inflame the situation. However, that night there were roses on my doorstep," she tells Lenny. "And every night after that . . . until . . . until . . ."

"Until what?" Lenny says gently.

Claire looks at him desperately. "It escalated so fast . . ." she says through gasping dry sobs, her body beginning to relive the trauma. "I just had no idea that Ryan was deranged, or I would have done something much earlier. I would have gone to the police . . ."

"You're still not telling me what happened?" Lenny persists.

Claire takes one more swallow to try to ease her dry throat and help her get through the next few moments. Then she says, "Two weeks after the first night he followed us home, Ryan murdered Todd."

She stops and watches the last vestiges of color drain from Lenny's face.

chapter seventeen

LENNY

There is a long, long silence as Lenny struggles desperately to find the right thing to say. "Oh my god, Claire, I'm so, so sorry," he tries eventually, ignoring the cascade of questions he really wants to ask, because she looks utterly broken as she sits in front of him, as though her loss is still unbearably raw.

They're both silent for a while, staring into the gloom of the room. Lenny wants to wrap his arms around Claire, but he's worried it's the wrong gesture, too intimate, and she might close down if he tries. So he keeps his distance and waits.

Eventually, she begins talking again. "I found out a lot of things about Ryan afterward, during the trial. He was a well-known drug dealer with a god complex, and he'd already had a few stints in jail for dealing and violent conduct. Plenty of people testified that he was basically unhinged, but no one had done anything to stop him before it was too late." She pauses for a moment. "That's probably unfair—how could anyone have predicted what he might do? He was psychotic."

Lenny's heart pounds in his chest. "Claire, please tell me he's in jail. That you're not thinking he's found us."

He sees something pass across Claire's face as he says the word *us*. "He was sentenced to life," she says, "but I've always been terrified that he would get out somehow and come after me. He blamed me, you know. He ranted in court that it was my fault for leading him on—even said he thought I had evil powers and had bewitched him." She gets up and goes across to pour herself a glass of water, taking her time, as Lenny's mind races with all the horrors of everything he's heard. As she sits back down, clutching the drink, she says, "Because of everything that's been happening, I've hardly been able to focus on anything. So I got in touch with my old caseworker Mary-Rose earlier today, and earlier tonight Mary-Rose called to tell me Ryan isn't in Paremoremo anymore—that's the high-security prison in New Zealand where he's serving life—and no one will tell her where he's gone."

Lenny feels sucker-punched for the umpteenth time. "But . . . I don't understand. Surely no one in their right mind would let him go free?"

"I don't think so either," Claire says quietly. "And Mary-Rose is certain they wouldn't release him. I'm hanging my last threads of sanity onto her words, but if it's not him, who's sending the texts? And those flowers?" She gestures at the kitchen counter. "The message doesn't feel like a coincidence— the roses he used to leave on my doorstep always had the same note: *From a secret admirer.* And the texts you've been getting, there's no subtlety in them, is there? Whoever it is, they want us to know they won't give up—which is exactly how Ryan would behave. Even after he was in jail, I'd get anonymous messages, telling me to watch my back. It's what I've always been most frightened of—that he would come back and mess with my life again and try to hurt the people I love. It's why I didn't just leave New Zealand . . . I faked my own death."

Lenny gapes. Just when he thinks there can't possibly be more, there's another bombshell. "You faked your death?" he splutters eventually.

"I didn't see where I had a choice, because I kept getting threats even after Ryan was convicted—more flowers, and notes telling me my family would be next. Mary-Rose supported me—even once he was locked up, we feared he had too many contacts that might be willing to do a job for him. I faked my suicide, and she contacted my family once I'd gone, told them I was safe and well, but that it was better for everyone if I didn't return and they didn't tell anyone or try to find me while Ryan was still alive."

Lenny gapes at her. "Shit."

The puzzle surrounding Claire suddenly rearranges itself into a series of realizations. "So this is why you've withdrawn from me? In case it happens again. To me? Or the kids? But, Claire, why didn't you just tell me?"

"Because I didn't think you deserved to spend your life constantly looking over your shoulder because of me," Claire answers quietly. "I can tell you firsthand that it's a terrible way to live. I've always known Ryan has connections with some pretty dangerous people, and I still don't know how far he'll go to find me. He's a total psycho, and I couldn't bear to bring that into our marriage. Otherwise, what was the point of leaving, if I can never escape him and his threats? Besides, I didn't think I'd ever have a life like this—partly because I don't feel I deserve it when someone else is dead because of me. And also because it's terrifying, loving you all, knowing what could happen because of my chance encounter with a madman." She shudders.

Lenny swallows hard, "So what do we do now?" he asks. "Christ, how did we get here? I don't know how you're managing to talk about it so calmly, after all you've been through."

She tilts her head, considering the question. "I'm not calm—but in some ways, I've been expecting it. Devon taught me that some people never give up on trying to get revenge."

"The guy from the beach?" Lenny asks, remembering the way the man had jumped him; how protective he had been. "How does he fit into all this?"

"Mary-Rose put me in touch with him, and he helped me build a life here. He got me a false ID. Trained me in self-defense. He's a former policeman, but he left the force after his sister was stalked for years and then killed by her ex-husband ten years after she left him. The guy finally lost it, cornered her in the parking lot of the accountancy firm she worked for, and stabbed her to death. The police had done nothing to help, despite her begging them so many times. After umpteen court orders and so many evasive measures she lost count. His determination to take her life was greater than all of that in the end. That's why Devon's made it his life's work to try to stop it from happening to any more women. Since then, he's has taken on women like me and looks after us; training us mentally and physically to cope with what we've been through and the possibility of being stalked again. He doesn't always do things according to the law because his main objective is to keep us alive," she says. "And he's had failures as well as success."

Lenny is lost for words, gaping at Claire, struggling to grasp the magnitude of horror that kind of harassment brought, and the futility of everything they'd tried to stop it. Instinctively, he looks back at the flowers and his head swims.

Claire stands up and puts a hand on his shoulder. "Look, we have to do this one step at a time. Let's go to bed, and when we get up you can focus on the gig, and I'll try to get my lunchtime classes covered. I'd already canceled the others to handle the kids and give you some space."

"I can't do the gig like this," Lenny objects.

"I think you have to," Claire insists. "We can't let whoever this is win. We can't let them chase us into hiding. And this is an opportunity you've been wanting for a long time. No one can replace you at this stage, so everyone will miss out if we let them down."

Lenny sighs. "I guess you're right. But surely it can't be Ryan who's messing with us. They wouldn't just release someone from prison—certainly not without telling the victims."

Claire grimaces. "The only problem with that is that the victim was Lucy Rutherford, who faked her own suicide, and has therefore been presumed dead for over a decade."

They fall quiet, processing the implications of what she's just said, until Claire stands up. "I'm sorry, Lenny, but I'm so exhausted I feel like I'm about to pass out, and my head is throbbing. Reliving this is as unbearable as it's always been—I don't think it'll ever get easier. I have to lie down and at least try to get some rest," she says, then pauses before adding, "you should too."

Their eyes lock. "I think I'll stay up for a bit," he says.

Claire touches his hand tentatively, a small stroke of comfort—or perhaps an apology—before she disappears, leaving him sitting in the dark, alone with his thoughts.

He stays like that for a long time before he pulls his phone out of his pocket and messages Dave.

"Can you call me in the morning, first thing?" he texts. "I need your help."

chapter eighteen

CLAIRE

"Y̶ou're taking us to school?" Jake asks in astonishment. "Is Dad okay?"

"He's just having a lie-in—his band is playing tonight, remember," Claire says, sipping her coffee and hoping she can clear some of the fog in her brain before she has to go out. As soon as she'd heard the alarm, she'd reminded Lenny to stay in bed, that she'd do the school run, and he'd mumbled his appreciation and rolled over. She wants to hang around and talk to him more about all she'd told him last night, but now isn't the time.

She'd woken up to another message from Elizabeth, apologizing for her dismissal and asking if they could talk. She hasn't responded yet but she doesn't want anything more to do with Jarrod and Elizabeth; she's just got to figure out how to get rid of them for good.

"So, what do you have in your packed lunches?" she asks the kids, going to the cupboard and looking through it. She turns around just in time to see Jake glancing at Emily and putting his fingers to his lips. "Dad always gives us two biscuits each."

"Is that right?" She grins, watching the challenge on their faces turn to glee as she goes to the cupboard and collects two shortbread cookies for each of them, nestling them next to the grapes.

It sets the stage for a contented, fuss-free morning, and she drives the kids to school feeling pleased with herself. She holds their hands as they walk across the playground to their classroom and leans down to give them a cuddle at the door.

"You have to come in with us, Mummy," Emily says, "until the bell rings."

"Oh." Claire looks around, a little embarrassed to need to be told, and finds that a few of the mums, none of whom she knows beyond a wave and a greeting, are observing them curiously. Most look away as soon as she makes eye contact, but as Emily drags Claire over to the reading corner, she notices Saskia sitting on a small plastic chair nearby, watching her. Saskia's expression isn't hostile, nor is it friendly, and Claire's heart sinks.

"Hi, Saskia," she says, kneeling on the mat while Emily looks for a book. To her right, Jake has joined the puzzle table with some of his friends and is busy completing a picture of a little red steam train.

"You've given Lenny the day off today then?" Saskia asks snippily.

Claire bites back a sarcastic retort, keen to keep it polite for the kids' sakes. "He's got the gig tonight, so he's having a lie-in."

"Right," Saskia says, getting up as the bell goes. "I might see you later then." She turns to say goodbye to her son and then makes her way out of the classroom. Claire gives Jake and Emily quick hugs and then races after her, calling out, "Saskia!"

Saskia turns, but as Claire gets closer, she can see that the other woman is trembling, her face red.

"I know what you're doing," Claire says, searching Saskia's expression, hoping to find answers, but biting back the question she really wants to ask. *Are you the one messing with us?* It suddenly seems crazy to be frightened of Ryan finding her all these years later, when Saskia is right here and so obviously vindictive.

"And what would that be?"

"I realize Lenny might leave me for you," Claire says quietly. "But you can't force him. You have to give him space to decide."

She sees the anger ripple through Saskia's body. "Why don't you just get out of his life?" Saskia bursts out, her voice high and tremulous. "You don't even want him." A few other mums making their way back toward their cars glance uncomfortably across at them.

Despite her best intentions to keep calm, Saskia's words needle Claire. "It's not like that, actually," she replies. "You don't know anything about me."

Saskia steps closer, her eyes alight with fury. "I know you and Lenny are over. You don't even want to sleep with him," she says. "He's only with you because of the kids. Well, I can take care of him—in every way," she adds pointedly.

Claire's entire body tenses. She leans into Saskia's face, and Saskia, who is a good few inches shorter, suddenly seems to realize that Claire is on the edge of self-control and strong enough to win a fight. Saskia's expression turns fearful. "What the hell does he see in you?" she asks Claire, her tone disgusted but her bottom lip wobbling, so that Claire can't tell whether she's being obnoxious or is simply hurt and heartsore.

Saskia breaks the moment, turning and hurrying away, and Claire walks quickly to her car, her thoughts running over everything that was said. She had mistakenly thought that Saskia was a distraction for Lenny, not a threat. But now she wonders how far the woman might go to get what she wants.

As she heads for home, she thinks over the text messages Lenny had shown her. If Saskia had looked into Claire's background, could she have found anything? It's hard to imagine so, but there's no one else who so obviously wants to split them up. In which case, Claire's glad she's begun confiding in Lenny, revealing her side of the story before it can be hijacked. Although there's a lot more she's yet to share. She hasn't told her husband about the awful trip to the courthouse to watch the end of Ryan's trial, after being persuaded that it might help her get closure. That it had been another terrible mistake, as Ryan had sought her out in the packed room, just after the verdict, while the chaotic atmosphere was still full of outrage and emotion. Out of everyone there, it had been her gaze he'd held for a moment before he was pulled away; and she hadn't needed to hear the words to know what he was saying, because she'd read it in his eyes: *I'm not done with you yet.* She'd known that he was telling her he could see right into her soul and find the stain there: the dark place inside her that would never disappear. He was conveying in one look that while he was guilty of an atrocity, so was she.

As Claire arrives home and parks in the driveway she takes long deep breaths, doing her utmost to withstand the cascade of threatening thoughts. She glances at the house opposite her own, its calm, quiet facade seeming to mock her. Her adrenaline is still firing from the brief confrontation in the schoolyard, but perhaps her energy would be better served by confronting her new neighbor. Because although Saskia obviously wants Claire and Lenny to split up, Tilly is the one making oblique mentions of places Claire desperately wants to forget.

Before she can lose courage, she hurries across to the road and knocks on the door of number twelve.

A man she's never seen before answers. He's tall, with a shaven head and an earring, and wears a vest top and board shorts. He looks her up and down without smiling.

"You must be Gary," Claire says quickly. "I'm Claire, your neighbor." She gestures across at her own house, then holds out her hand.

Gary doesn't take it, just regards it with a smirk. "Tilly, our neighbor's come for a visit," he calls behind him, before disappearing back inside.

Tilly appears at the door moments later, sporting jeans and a hoodie. Despite the fact it's still early, she's already wearing tons of makeup, and she flashes Claire her familiar red-lipsticked grin. "Morning, neighbor, what can I do for you?"

"Can I come in and talk to you for a moment?" Claire asks without returning the pleasantries.

Tilly looks intrigued. "Sorry, it's not a good time. Gary's getting ready for work. Can we talk out here? Or I could come over to yours?"

"No, Lenny's still in bed," Claire says, "and the thing is . . ." She pauses, wishing they weren't doing this on the doorstep, but then again perhaps it's better that they're in public view.

"You mentioned a place called Silverlakes the other night, and I used to know some folks there. You mean the town near Hamilton, right? I wondered how long you lived there—if we might know some of the same people? I haven't spoken to anyone there in a long time. It would be nice to reminisce."

She's not sure what she'd expected as a result of directly calling Tilly's bluff, but it isn't the smile that spreads across Tilly's face.

"Oh, I wasn't there for long," she shrugs. "We were just passing through really. Didn't have time to meet many people. But hey," she adds, "those flowers you got yesterday were lovely. Must have cost a bit. Were they from Lenny, or do you have another secret admirer on the scene?" She winks.

Utterly confused by the turn of the conversation, Claire is lost for a reply. "I have no idea who they're from. I suspect they got the wrong address," she says, still surveying Tilly intently.

"Maybe Lenny's got a secret admirer," Tilly suggests, a glint in her eye. "There was another woman hanging about the other day while you were out. Pretty lady with curly hair and big boobs, dresses like a gypsy. You know her?"

"Lenny's friends with lots of the school mums," Claire replies steadily, holding her gaze. "Thanks for the chat, but I should go—I'll catch you later."

"Tell Lenny I'm coming to watch him sing at the pub tonight," Tilly calls out after her as Claire hurries across to the house. "I can't wait."

Lenny greets her just inside the front door, still in his pajamas. "I saw you talking to Tilly. What happened? Did you discover anything?"

Claire is still trying to process the conversation. "No,

nothing. I don't know what I was expecting but she diverted my attention from talking about Silverlakes. Played it down. She's so weird, isn't she? And she made a point of telling me about seeing you and Saskia the other day. Oh, and that she's coming to your gig."

"Great," Lenny says, pushing his hand through his unbrushed hair as he heads toward the kitchen. "Just what I need."

"I don't understand her at all," Claire says, following him. "She's almost over-the-top friendly, but when I mentioned Silverlakes and went on the offensive, she brushed it off again. It's the place Ryan came from, and where . . . where Todd was killed. That's too much of a coincidence, surely? Although I did check the stats and there are ten thousand people living there now, which is more than I thought." Claire collects a bottle of water out of the fridge as she talks and pours herself a glass. "Either she knows something and is being deliberately vague, or she knows absolutely nothing, and therefore doesn't understand why I'm asking."

"And let's not forget that I was getting the texts before she arrived," Lenny reminds her.

"Yes, although she could have begun sending them before she moved here. But there's no obvious connection with her, other than place . . . and I was thinking about it all again on the way home." She pauses, and sees Lenny tense, as though he already senses what she's thinking. "I'd assumed all this was connected to Ryan," Claire says, "but what if someone else is involved, trying to make sure we split up? All the things that have happened are designed to make you doubt me." She hesitates. "Could Saskia be behind this?"

"I really don't think so," Lenny replies quickly.

Claire bristles. "She was pretty testy in the schoolyard this morning, suggesting you're only staying here because of the kids. You must know how badly she wants you. There's nothing she'd like more than to split us up, and if she had even a hint of the things I told you last night, I'm sure she'd use them against me."

"Saskia's not like that," Lenny insists. "She's not vindictive." But he looks uncertain.

"I just think we need all options on the table," Claire persists, trying to loosen his conviction further while she has the chance. "Don't you?"

For a moment she thinks he'll object again, but then he relents. "Okay. But I still don't think it's her."

"She wants you more than you realize," Claire says quietly. "The way she looks at me, I can tell. She thinks you're hers already, and I'm in the way."

She wants him to deny it, but instead she watches Lenny's face blanch as he acknowledges the truth of her words.

chapter nineteen

LENNY

As soon as Claire has left for the arena, Lenny grabs his phone. Dave had replied to Lenny's message first thing, saying he would be around all morning to talk, and although Lenny doesn't like asking for favors, this time he's desperate.

"We've had a few strange things going on here," Lenny explains once they've said their hellos. "I've been getting texts from an anonymous number for a couple of weeks now, accusing Claire of lying to me. And then yesterday a bunch of flowers were left on the doorstep, addressed to Claire, from "a secret admirer." And the thing is, I found a sticker on the bottom of the box they came in." He's glad Dave can't see him cringing as he works up to his request. "It looks like they were bought at a local shop, Lakeland Flowers, and I wondered if you could find out who purchased them." He stops and waits for Dave to either laugh at him or hang up, sure that he's overstepping a boundary by even asking.

There's a protracted pause before Dave replies. "Bloody hell, Lenno, you're full of surprises this week, aren't you? It's not technically allowed, mate, but since it's so close, I'll swing by in uniform on my way to the bar and ask a few questions at the shop, see what information they volunteer. No harm in that, but I can't make any promises."

Lenny almost tells him not to worry about it, but then stops himself. If this can help them uncover who is intruding into their lives, he really wants to know. "If you can, that would be great." He looks at the bouquet sitting innocently on the countertop. "It's twelve red roses arranged in a vase with a red ribbon."

"I don't suppose they sell hundreds of those a day," Dave replies. "I'll see what I can do."

Once they've hung up, Lenny makes himself a drink and takes it back to bed, still mulling over the conversation. While Dave had been kind enough to play it down and act like this was a normal request, he was obviously bemused by the whole situation. It's going to be pretty embarrassing if this is some kind of ruse and Claire really does have a secret admirer; if somehow all this is one enormous lie to cover an affair. But even as he thinks it, he's sure he's clutching at straws. Claire would have to be a complete sociopath to come up with a detailed story like the one she'd told him last night. It doesn't fit with anything he knows about her. She's never been attention-seeking or manipulative; and even though she keeps her head down and is always preoccupied with work, she's never cold either. She acts like all she really wants is to be left alone so she can fly under the radar; that fits completely with what he's just learned about her.

Nevertheless, he can't help himself, as he begins to look up all the names and events that Claire had mentioned last night. In Google, he types in the names Ryan and Lucy Rutherford, and the browser instantly displays a series of stories about the conviction of Ryan Doherty for murdering rising track star Todd Langdon, and the devastating suicide of teenager Lucy Rutherford, who'd been caught up in the tragedy. A few of the news pages have pictures of young Lucy, who looks quite different from Claire with her long blond hair and the fringe that sweeps across the top of her eyebrows, but is still unmistakably his wife, with her apple cheeks and dimpled smile.

However, as Lenny reads, his heart begins to race again, because Claire has left out one key element in her retelling:

"Rising Track Star Todd Langdon Killed in Front of his Girlfriend."

"Girlfriend Forced to Watch as Stalker Kills Athlete Todd Langdon."

She was there.

The realization is yet another crippling blow. *Why had she left this part out?* he wonders, reading on.

Ryan Doherty was convicted yesterday for the murder of rising athletics star Todd Langdon, after the judge rejected the plea of insanity. Langdon was tortured with a knife and then stabbed multiple times in front of his girlfriend Lucy Rutherford in June 2011, after Doherty became obsessed with Rutherford and spent weeks stalking her. Sentencing is expected next month.

For god's sake, Lenny, he berates himself. Of course she didn't tell him—why would she want to relive that?

He's about to close the browser when he notices another news article about Lucy's suicide. The accompanying picture shows her family gathered in a huddle at the cliff top where their beloved Lucy was last seen, their faces crumpled by the agony of their grief. He wonders if they had known at that point that she was still alive? If so, it's a convincing display of despair. But then again, they had still lost her, hadn't they?—not to death, but it would have felt almost as final and distressing.

He's looking at Jake and Emily's grandmother, he thinks with another shock. And their uncle and aunt. He can even see an echo of his children in these people's faces. He can't believe he hasn't looked up her family before: but she'd said they'd been awful and disowned her, and he'd felt it would be disloyal to pursue it.

He'd felt angry with Claire last night, for what he saw as a deceit; but these strangers' faces bring home the extent of the tragedy for all of them. He rubs his forehead, holding back the emotion that threatens to overwhelm him. Why hadn't he asked Claire more about her past over the years? He could have tried to gently coax the story from her—he'd known it was something traumatic. Why had he ignored it, and let her push him away?

The world Lenny is suddenly caught up in is gnawing hard at his gut. In the police photos Ryan looks crazed, his eyes fierce and bulging, his stare cold and unflinching. It wasn't the picture of a man who was ashamed of what he'd done; instead, he emanated a cold, evil fury. By all accounts Ryan was a madman, but the reporting on him went cold as soon as he was sentenced, and Lenny wants to know more. What had he been like in prison? And where the hell is he now? He needs to research the details for himself, so he can be sure they are all safe, because one aspect of this new reality keeps on hitting him: if Ryan is still deranged, Lenny might well be directly in his new line of sight.

By the time he stops scrolling and checks the clock he's surprised to see it's past ten, and he isn't even dressed. He scrambles up, aware that he only has this morning to fix the stupid hole in the wall, and despite Joanna's instructions, he's still not confident that he's going to be able to do it properly. He's done plenty of dodgy filler jobs in his time, trying to cover up nail holes and ending up with dimpled uneven surfaces and unimpressed landlords. And this isn't an easy repair: Jake had made an impressive dent with the bat.

He gets up reluctantly, and once dressed he heads out to purchase what he needs, returning an hour later with filler and scraper. Like all DIY jobs, when he begins doing it, he wonders why it's taken him so long: the job isn't as bad as it looks, and within an hour he has applied the quick-dry filler and painted over it. The color seems to match the wall well enough, although he won't know for sure until it's dry. He stretches out his lower back, stiff and uncomfortable from working on his knees. Although he'd laid a towel down to serve as a cushion on the cold tile floor, his kneecaps are objecting too, bruised and sore.

He uses the nearby TV cabinet to help himself get to his feet and as he does so he glances at the TV. At the back of it, there's a maze of crisscrossing wires connecting to Jake's Nintendo box, a set-top box, and a DVD player they hardly ever use. But he catches sight of a tiny loop of wire that appears stuck to the underneath and ends in a little disk of black attached so it's almost invisible against another one of the hanging wires.

He draws closer to examine it, but at the sight of a microscopic little eye, he recoils as though it might release a poisoned dart straight at him. He stares at it for a moment, aware of his short, uneven breaths, and then leans forward and plucks it from the wire it's attached to. It comes away but there's some sort of sticky glue on the back of it, and he sees the wire leads to a very small battery pack. He pulls the battery out, and throws the camera onto the floor, ready to stamp on it until he realizes he might be destroying evidence. He goes over to the kitchen and puts the little spycam in an opaque Tupperware box that features Woody and Buzz Lightyear giving him the thumbs-up. Then he calls Claire, speaking in a rush as soon her voice mail message comes on.

"You have to call me straightaway. I think I just found a hidden camera in our house."

chapter twenty

CLAIRE

When Claire arrives home, Lenny is waiting for her outside.

She gets out of the car and hurries over to him, lowering her voice to a whisper. "There's really a camera in there?"

He blows out a breath. "Yep, and I'm not keen to go inside and talk about it if there are more of them spying on us."

Claire eyes the house opposite. "You really think we should talk about it out here."

Lenny follows her gaze and snaps, "For fuck's sake," before he marches back into the house. In the kitchen, he grabs the Tupperware and thrusts it at Claire. "This is what I found underneath the TV."

She opens the container and looks at the tiny piece of equipment in there. Her lip trembles, thinking of someone watching them all. The kids. The tensions and arguments. Their conversation last night. She works hard to control herself. This isn't the moment to fall apart.

"I've pulled the wires out," he says. "I'd quite like to stamp on it but I don't want to destroy evidence."

"This is bad." She looks around the house, eyes darting quickly across surfaces, wondering how many more there are. "When the lizard disappeared, and you said you misplaced the keys for a while, I tried to dismiss it as a weird mix-up." She hesitates. "But now I'm genuinely scared that someone can get in and out of the house."

"Yep, me too. I'm going to call Dave and ask how we get the police involved."

"No," she says quickly. "Devon will be better. Let me call him instead."

Lenny looks at her aghast. "Claire, someone is spying on us. Are you really saying we shouldn't go to the police?"

"Lenny, were you not listening to anything I said last night?" Claire is trying hard not to raise her voice but she can't keep the emotion and frustration out of it. "I had to leave everything behind because it was obvious the police couldn't protect me. And I'm not blaming them—it's ridiculous to think they'd have enough time to provide me with my personal bodyguard. But I'm not unrealistic about what they can do either. If Ryan is somehow behind all this, I have to protect us—and Devon is the best person to help." She's already texting as she talks.

Lenny storms off to the bedroom and Claire follows. She wants to go and check the gun, which is hidden in her underwear drawer, but she doesn't dare under the circumstances, so she begins to take off her jacket and shoes. "I've canceled or covered my classes for a few days. I'm due for some sick days, so I can help out here. I'll wait for Devon so you can go and practice."

Lenny sits down heavily beside her on the bed. "I can't even think about the gig at the moment," he says. "I might be able to pull out of it, find someone else. Dave's friend Lucas would probably jump at the chance."

"No way," Claire says. "I took the days off so you could keep going. Devon will help. We're going to find out what's happening and fix it, okay?"

"I don't understand how you can be so calm."

"I'm not calm. But Devon taught me enough to be ready for this moment, if it came." She casts a discreet glance toward her chest of drawers but says nothing more. She doesn't want to dwell on Lenny's probable reaction if she tells him there's a loaded gun in the house.

Lenny sounds nervous when he speaks again. "I looked a few things up this morning. About Ryan, and your family . . ."

She turns to him quickly and holds up her hand. "I wish you hadn't. Please don't say any more. In eleven years, I've never typed their names into a search bar, because it felt too dangerous for them and too traumatic for me. I cannot deal with everything at once, okay? Let's sort out our own problems first before we talk about my family again." Her voice cracks on the last words. "Can you imagine how much I've missed them? How much I've missed out on, and vice versa?" she adds in a pained whisper. "All because of one sadistic bastard."

He comes to sit beside her. "I'm sorry, I'm a prick. I didn't mean to upset you."

Claire can't deal with any more emotion right now. She checks her phone. "Devon says he'll be here within the hour:

he'll know how to help. Hang tight, okay." She pats his hand. "And please know that I never intended to bring the horrors of my past into yours or the kids' lives."

Lenny puts his elbows on his knees and steeples his fingers before leaning his chin on them and blowing out a breath. "You don't need to be sorry: you're the victim here. I've only ever wanted to support you, Claire. I know we made our vows in an Elvis chapel and not a court of law, but I thought that was just more our style, not because we were fooling around. I still meant every word. The idea wasn't that you continued going through everything alone. We're supposed to be a team."

Claire flinches. "I know," she says. "I meant it too. But I never imagined how hard it would be with the kids. I love them, but I'm frightened for them *all* the time. I'm really grateful you're so good with them . . ."

"But I'm not," Lenny laughs. "Mum rescues me regularly. I'm overwhelmed, too, and depressed at the thought of not being able to give them everything I want them to have. I hate being so useless, and unable to financially provide like you can. Besides, have you seen the way Emily looks at you . . . ? You're her hero."

"The way Emily looks at me is terrifying, Len," Claire says. "It's a continual reminder of everything I might lose. I've always been frightened that Ryan will come back. That I might have to leave, and they would never understand why. I've always known that Ryan wouldn't care how little they were: he'd see them as nothing else but ammunition to hurt me. While it was just us two I could—"

She's interrupted by a knock on the door. "That'll be

Devon," she says, as Lenny jumps up to look out of the window. "He was fast."

"Shit," Lenny says, turning away. "It's not Devon, it's the bloody estate agent—I fixed the wall this morning because she wanted to check it today while she's visiting the neighbors."

Claire looks intrigued. "We should ask her about them while she's here. See what she knows."

"I'm not sure she'll tell us anything," Lenny says. "She's a bit snooty and I doubt it's policy."

But Claire has already jumped off the bed and gone to let her in. Lenny can hear them talking in the corridor.

"Nice to see *you* today," Joanna says to Claire, then looks pointedly at Lenny. He remembers that it was Saskia whom she'd encountered the last time and is immediately embarrassed, hoping Joanna doesn't say more.

"Okay, Joanna, the paint might still be a bit wet," Lenny says, "but I've done it." He walks through to the lounge and gestures at the wall.

"Great, thank you, it's nice to finally tick that one off," Joanna says, looking around. "And I told you I got permission for the lizard to stay, didn't I?"

"Lenny mentioned it," Claire says eagerly. "We're very grateful for that. Jake adores him." She pauses for a moment, and Lenny can see her weighing her words. "We were wondering, actually, if it's possible to get the locks changed?"

Joanna swings around. "Why do you ask that?"

"We . . . we think someone might have access to the house. Some things have moved around or gone missing."

"Really?" Joanna looks shocked. "What kind of things?"

Claire and Lenny glance at one another. "The lizard

disappeared for a bit," Lenny says, annoyed to feel himself redden. "And a couple of other things have moved around in the TV area."

Joanna looks concerned but tries to laugh it off. "You're sure you're not just both getting forgetful? Kids do that to you, you know."

"It's not that," Claire snaps. "Lenny found a small camera under the television—we think someone's spying on us."

Joanna looks startled. "Really?" She glances around uncertainly. "That's troubling."

"Yes, and the new neighbors are acting a bit strangely too," Claire bursts out.

Joanna turns to her. "Oh? What are they doing?"

Claire thinks fast. Now, as she's asked to outline what the neighbors have done, all she can think of is: they were friendly, and the woman came over with a bottle of wine, complimented us, and mentioned a place they used to live that I recognized. It's hardly damning stuff. And there's nothing to say Tilly actually stole the lizard or planted a camera in the house.

So she stands there like a fool, and Lenny takes over. "They had a big row when they first arrived, and they don't seem to get on that well. The woman, Tilly, is nice enough, but she can be overfamiliar. And the guy is a bit aggressive."

Joanna looks unsure. "Oh dear. Well, moving can be stressful. Let's hope they settle down. I'll head there now as I need to go over a few contractual bits and pieces. If they give you any trouble, call the office and let me know."

"Where were they living before this?" Claire asks.

Joanna makes for the door. "I'm not really supposed to divulge details about clients. Why don't you have a chat with them and see if you can get to know them a bit more?"

She rushes for the door, obviously unsettled by their questions. They see her out, and once she's gone, Lenny turns to Claire. "I knew exactly why you stalled when she asked what they were up to. We're not sure Tilly has done anything except be exceptionally friendly. Are we going crazy?"

"No," Claire says, "but perhaps someone wants us to feel like we are."

Lenny sighs, running a hand over his mouth. "I still don't feel like Tilly or Saskia are behind all this. And Ryan sounds terrifying, but surely, they wouldn't release him on the quiet after what he did. I keep searching for another explanation."

His words set Claire's mind racing. She hesitates, then decides they need to consider every possibility, however much of a long shot it seems to be. "Actually, I've been having a problem with the husband of one of my clients—Jarrod Lynch. He turned up at the arena yesterday and insisted I train him. He offered me a lot of money. It's obvious he wants sex, but I'm not sure how far he'll go to get it. The thing is, he's the CEO of Shipman and Fine, and he even dangled the idea of a rent reduction as a carrot to let him seduce me. Surely, he'd be able to get access to the house?"

"What? You've got to be kidding," Lenny growls with a rush of fury. "How . . . how dare he!"

Claire shakes her head. "I know. He resorted to threats pretty fast. I think he sees women like goods on a shelf, there to be taken as desired, or for the right price."

Lenny gestures toward the flowers. "Well, surely Jarrod's a more likely candidate than a ghost from your past. We could go for a restraining order if that's the case." They fall silent as Claire considers this, then Lenny checks his watch. "Shit, I'm supposed to be at the Oceanside in half an hour."

Claire nods. "Then go. It's okay. I've got it covered. Devon will help us check the house, and after that it's only the school run. Go and get ready."

Lenny hesitates, but then turns toward the bedroom, and only once he's gone does Claire release the shudder she's been holding in. She glances around at the house, desperate to figure out who is behind all this, wondering just how long their adversary has been watching them.

chapter twenty-one

LENNY

Lenny is the first bandmember to arrive at the Oceanside. He grabs a drink and sits at a table in the corner, trying to steady his nerves, appreciating the leisurely feel of this time of the afternoon. The bar staff move slowly, wiping glasses and carrying crates of drinks between the storeroom and bar. The few people at tables are either solo drinkers with laptops in front of them, or sit in groups of twos and threes, all relaxed and taking their time. The TV banks above the bar and in the corners of the room are showing a golf tournament. There's enough ease in the room to make Lenny's problems feel slightly absurd rather than pressing.

He goes over and over the past few days, trying to apply some sort of logic to decoding who is really behind the phone messages; the flowers; the hidden camera. Even Bob's strange disappearance. He checks his phone to find there's no word from Claire yet. If Devon finds more cameras, he wants them to leave the house as soon as the gig is over. His mother, always ready to help, will surely take them in while they figure out the next steps.

He's sitting opposite the stage on one of the high-backed padded seats that run along the wall, and he stares at the empty space with its raised platform, trying to picture the band there tonight, playing up a storm. He closes his eyes and imagines himself lost in the music, taking his focus away from the nerves that come with a hundred or so people watching and assessing their performance, instead picturing the audience singing along to some of the classic hits. He begins to relax. They can do this—they're ready. They sound great in rehearsals, and their arguments are petty and perfectionist. Short of a sudden sore throat, there's nothing to worry about here.

Dave comes into the bar, wearing a sports jacket and jeans. He glances around, catches sight of Lenny, and hurries over with obvious purpose. "I'm glad you're here first," he says, pulling a stool across to sit opposite. "I was hoping for a private word."

There's an intensity to him that makes Lenny sit up. "Is everything all right?"

"Yeah, yeah." Dave scratches his cheek absent-mindedly. "I just wanted to let you know that I went to the flower shop for you."

Lenny's shoulders tense. "You found out who bought them?"

Dave laughs uncomfortably. "Yeah. I showed my badge and asked if I could see a record of yesterday's sales. Didn't take long, they'd sold less than twenty arrangements."

"And?"

"And Claire sent them to herself," Dave says, leaning back, pursing his lips, his expression concerned and sympathetic.

"What?" Lenny asks with an abrupt exhale of breath.

"She paid for them with her credit card. It was the only request for a dozen roses they had yesterday. She ordered them over the phone just after lunch."

"That doesn't make any sense." Lenny's brain is scrambling, trying to unravel this new twist.

"Actually, mate, I think it does," Dave says.

"What do you mean?"

"You and Saskia? All the school gossip? Claire wants to make you jealous."

Lenny doesn't bother to hide his disbelief. "Not likely."

"Don't be an idiot. She's still your wife, Lenny, even if she has, inexplicably, given you the green light to shag around. She probably didn't realize how it would feel until you actually went and did it," Dave adds. "Why the hell else would she send herself flowers from an anonymous admirer? She's unsettling you and cheering herself up at the same time. Don't tell me you didn't have a little spark of jealousy when you saw them?"

Lenny gapes at Dave. *It's true*, he thinks. *I hated the thought of someone wanting her enough to send her a huge bunch of roses. I couldn't stand it when she told me about Jarrod propositioning her. I'm jealous as hell, even though I have no idea if she still wants me.*

Dave is watching him, utterly baffled. "Mate, what is going on with you? I've never seen someone so happy as when you got together with Claire. What the hell happened?"

"The kids . . ." Lenny admits despondently. "It changed things between us. I . . . I don't think she really wanted them to begin with. Well, maybe that's a bit harsh, but the pregnancy wasn't planned, and when we had them, she couldn't cope."

Dave blows out a long breath. "I can understand that. It's

tough having one newborn, let alone twins. But maybe you guys need to fight a bit harder to stay together. The kids need you, they're the ones who will suffer if you blow your marriage up. Unless you truly love Saskia now?"

"I . . . she's . . ." Lenny can't seem to find the words.

"That's what I thought," Dave says. "It's always been Claire, hasn't it?"

"But the thing is," Lenny continues, growing more animated, waving his hands so that he almost sends Dave's drink flying, "I don't get why I feel so disconnected from Saskia. She makes me laugh, she's heaps of fun, and she's . . . it's good when we, you know . . . but I suppose I never thought it was anything serious. And the more I think about some of her behavior, the more she seems way too intense."

"Well, the heart wants what the heart wants," Dave says, shrugging. "You and Claire have always been a lot more than fun. You've never been able to take your eyes off her when she walks into a room."

Lenny stares down into his drink. "I know." Then he adds, "Shit!" loudly, making a few other afternoon punters briefly turn in their direction. He looks up at Dave. "She really sent them to herself?"

"Yep," Dave says, "but whatever's happening right now, the show must go on. So let's go, Freddie Mercury, we need to get focused and do our final checks. We all want to impress Baz; otherwise, tonight's gonna be the start and finish of our reunion."

They head into the back room, and within ten minutes Eddie and Fletcher have joined them. They check the equipment and the running schedule and practice a few of the trickier songs. Lenny's glad he's so confident in the set, because he can't seem to concentrate on anything properly, and he's aware of a few irritated mutters among his friends when he misses a beat and stuffs up a song.

As they finish, the conversation moves on to who's coming tonight, and then into full-blown reminiscences of other gigs years ago, each man's eyes alight as he goes back to his former glory days. Lenny tries to join in, but he might as well be locked in a clear glass box for all the distance he feels between their unbridled excitement and his unfettered nerves. He can't stop thinking about Claire. She'd acted so shocked when she saw the flowers and read the card. She'd used it as a catalyst to tell him about Ryan, but had that been a setup? If so, how easily she'd manipulated the situation, when she's been holding back from him for years. It all leads back to the same disturbing question.

When he's been in the dark for so long, how much can he really trust his wife?

chapter twenty-two

CLAIRE

"Thanks for taking the time to help us," Claire says as Devon puts his bag in the car. "I'm sorry to get you all the way out here for nothing."

"It's not nothing." Devon frowns. "I'm glad we didn't find anything more, but that doesn't change the fact there was a hidden camera and microphone in your lounge, Claire." He looks back at the house. "Where've you put the gun?"

"In my underwear drawer."

Devon catches her eye and raises his eyebrows, bemusement lifting the corners of his lips.

She shrugs. "I thought it was as good a place as any. Easy to reach, too high for the kids to bother with, and not somewhere Lenny will check."

He nods. "Yeah, okay, I see your thinking. But you should keep it with you. You can't protect yourself if you don't have it. So, what's the plan now?"

She sighs. "I think Lenny will want us to stay with his mum for a bit while we figure out what's going on. She's coming over tonight to babysit, so I'll have to try to talk to her. God knows what I'll say." She glances at the redbrick house across the road. "I need to find out more about Tilly since we can't really escape her while she's living across the road. Today is difficult. Lenny's got a gig at the Oceanside tonight that might lead to a decent job opportunity, and I was planning to be there for moral support, cheer him on and all that, but under the circumstances, I think I'd better stay here."

Devon hesitates for so long that Claire asks, "What are you thinking?"

"Look, if you were going to go to the gig," he says, "why don't you do that and take what's in your undie drawer—in case either you or Lenny need protection. I can stay here and sit outside, just in case."

Claire doesn't reply for a moment. The suggestion is surreal. Can they really be in so much danger that Devon is suggesting she take a gun to the local pub's band night? But whoever is behind the disturbing events of late, she has no idea whether they'll go further, or when. Perhaps Devon's right.

"I could do," she says, "but I'm not sure how we'll explain that to Lenny's mum when she comes to babysit. We'll freak her out one way or another—she'll either be frightened or think we're crazy."

"Then let's not tell her, if it's going to scare her. I'll drive around the block then park down the road, keep an eye on the house till you're home. She won't even need to know."

"You don't have to do that."

"I know I don't. I'm offering. It'll give you peace of mind, and my only plan tonight was Netflix and beer—they'll wait for a few hours. Keeping you safe is a bit more important, don't you think?"

She goes silent, thinking it through. "Thank you," she says eventually. "It'll only be a couple of hours—I think their set is for ninety minutes, so it won't be a late one."

"No problem. I'll go and grab a drive-thru and be back outside in about an hour." He pats the top pocket of his checked shirt, pulls out his tobacco and cigarette papers, and starts rolling. "You do what you need to do."

Claire goes inside, grabs her own keys, and heads off to school. The kids have been stuck in the after-school club for a couple of hours and are unimpressed that she's nearly fifteen minutes late and they're the last to leave. Nevertheless, Claire's grateful to have missed the possibility of school gossip or judgmental stares from the other parents.

Both Jake and Emily seem tired and are quiet on the ride home, and by the time they get back, Claire can see Devon's car parked at the end of the road. She's tempted to flash her lights in acknowledgment but knows he won't want that, so she ignores him and helps the kids out of the car instead. Jake runs in and turns the TV on straightaway, without asking, and Emily lies down next to him on the sofa. It's not the day for a skirmish about screentime, so Claire lets them get on with it and goes to rest on her bed for half an hour, closing her eyes in exhaustion and trying to momentarily block out all the worries the day has brought.

She desperately wants Lenny to do well at the gig tonight because he's sacrificed so many of his own interests for over five years now. She thinks about watching him perform and gets a nervous knot in her stomach, recalling all the times when they were first together and he had sung part of the song to her during his performances, with a wink or a smile. To be the recipient of his love and devotion had made her feel so different, giving her hope that she might one day live up to the person he appeared to see. But as the years went on, that had seemed an increasingly distant dream—one too painful to keep believing in. She's almost given up trying.

A knock on the door pulls her upright, and she goes straight to open it, expecting to find Lydia there, ready to babysit.

But it's Tilly waiting on the step, smiling brightly. "Hey, neighbor. Gary doesn't want to come to the pub tonight. Can I get a lift with you?"

"I . . ." Claire hesitates, but Tilly is beaming and seems nothing but friendly. Perhaps it's more strategic to keep her close and ask some questions. "I suppose so."

"Are you sure?" Tilly does a fake pout. "I don't want to put you out."

Claire shakes her head, trying to shrug off her unease. At least it means Tilly won't be at home, near Lydia and the kids.

"Sure, if you can come over at 6:45," she says. "It'll only take us ten minutes to get there, but I'd like to get a good spot if I can."

"Oh yay!" Tilly says, practically squealing with delight. "Our first girls' night out. See you shortly then." And she strides back across the road.

As soon as Claire closes the door, she gets a text from Devon.

Was that Tilly?

Yes.

Claire texts back.

> She wants to come with me to the gig.

> What did you say?

> I said I'll take her.

> Are you sure that's a good idea?

> No. But it felt like a better option than saying no. At least I'll know where she is.

> All right. But be careful, Claire. Stay alert and watch your back. Protect yourself.

> I will.

She sets the phone on the countertop, hoping that she's made the right decision, then goes to the drawer in the bedroom. She pulls out the Beretta and wraps it in a scarf, selecting one of her larger handbags, so she can slip the gun inside.

chapter twenty-three

LENNY

When they finish the final rehearsal, the band heads to Pappadillos, a local Italian restaurant. Fletcher and Eddie order huge pizzas and beers, but Lenny sticks to water and salad and Dave gets a side order of fries. Dave keeps giving Lenny concerned glances, perhaps more aware than the others that Lenny is checking his phone compulsively. Just as Fletcher and Eddie are finishing their ice cream sundaes, Lenny sees there are three messages waiting.

The first is from his mother, wishing him luck. And the second is from Claire.

Devon couldn't find anything else.

The news should calm his fears, but instead it compounds his confusion. If Claire lied about the flowers, then what else has she kept from him? Is Devon involved in the deceit? Are they taking Lenny for a fool?

However, it's the final text that leaves him struggling to resist hurling the phone at the wall.

> She's still lying to you, Lenny. Don't trust her.

Each little word curdles his blood. *Still lying.* As though someone knows about their heart-to-hearts this week.

Don't trust her.

And although he wants to hammer on the delete key until all those messages are gone, to dismiss them as nothing more than a vindictive troll having their fun, he can't stop the words from reverberating. Because after all he's learned during the past week, the truth is that he isn't sure who he's married to anymore.

He takes long, steadying breaths of fresh air as they walk back along the marina, heading into the pub's rehearsal room for the final time. The jokes die away and the four of them are all business now, fiddling with instruments, psyching themselves up. Fletcher disappears to do a last check of the drum kit, and they hear the murmur of the busy pub as the door opens. *This is it*, Lenny thinks. *Showtime.*

Pete the landlord pokes his head around the door. "Someone to see you, Eddie," he says. "Name's Baz. Can I let him in?"

"Sure, sure," Eddie says, in such a showy tone of bonhomie that the others struggle to suppress their amusement.

When Baz enters the room, he isn't at all how Lenny has pictured him. Tall and willowy, with a bald patch rimmed with fine brown hair and Harry Potter style glasses, he appears more like a meek accountant than a casino manager. He beams at them as Fletcher walks back in.

"Hey, fellas, I won't keep you. Just wanted to say how much I'm looking forward to this. Eddie has told me great things."

They each murmur their thanks and he gives them all a small salute before disappearing again. Lenny's not sure whether the visit was really necessary, but it has definitely moved his nerves up a notch, and he can see the others feel the same. Fletcher rolls his wrists and stretches out his fingers, and Eddie's face is bright red as he and Dave get back to tuning their guitars.

Lenny checks his phone again, to find another message from Claire.

> Devon's going to stay outside the
> house and keep watch, just in case,
> so I'll be there tonight. Probably not
> needed but it makes me feel better.
> Won't tell your mum as I don't want
> to scare her. I'll see you soon.

Lenny processes the message and then turns off his phone. There's nothing more he can do right now. It's time to focus on being a frontman for the next few hours and get this gig rolling.

chapter twenty-four

CLAIRE

"I'm sorry we've asked you to babysit so much this week," Claire says, as she stands there with her coat on and keys in hand, watching Lydia embrace the kids.

"Don't be silly," Lydia replies. She comes over and gives Claire a hug, which she always does, even though Claire's response is tepid at best. "Like I said to Lenny, they're my grandkids, not a chore. I love spending time with them. You go on and enjoy yourself."

"You're not leaving, are you, Nanna?" Emily asks, running over and grabbing Lydia around the waist.

"Nope, I'm staying so your mum can go and see your daddy singing, if you two aren't sick of me this week?" Lydia chuckles, to which the kids laugh and cry, "Nooo!"

Claire feels a twinge of envy, longing for Lydia's patience and easy manner. As Emily takes her Nanna's hand, there's a knock on the front door.

"Expecting someone?" Lydia frowns, her eyes flicking over to the roses, still sitting in their wrapper on the countertop. Claire wonders what she must be thinking about the flowers. Does her mother-in-law think she's having an affair? Perhaps that's why she's so eager for Claire to go to Lenny's gig. But there's no time for reassurance now.

"It'll be the new neighbor from across the road," Claire says. "She wants to go to see the band, and I said I'd give her a lift."

"Oh," Lydia's face relaxes again, "that's nice. Lenny seemed a bit worried about her, but I thought she was lovely. I'm glad you've made friends."

Claire doesn't respond to that. "See you later, kids," she calls out to Jake and Emily, going across to kiss the tops of their heads. Jake already has his eyes back on the TV, but Emily leans in for a proper hug. "Have a nice time, Mummy."

"Tell Daddy to break a leg," Jake says, turning to grin at her.

Claire laughs. "I will. I'm sure he'll appreciate that." She smiles at Lydia, and the tension eases between them, before Claire heads for the door.

Tilly waits by the front step, dressed in navy jeans and a smart white shirt. Her petite face is framed by her short-cropped hair, which is shiny and perfectly in place. Her skin is clear and pale; the few soft lines on her forehead are the only giveaway of her age.

"Hi Tilly, let's go," Claire says, hoping her smile appears genuine as they get into the car.

Tilly climbs into the passenger side. "You must be pretty excited," she says. "It's awesome to have a husband in a band."

"Lenny hasn't done a gig like this for years," Claire replies, starting the engine and beginning to reverse down the drive. "But I did used to love watching him sing."

As Tilly falls silent beside her, Claire is aware of how close they are to one another, and the overpowering smell of Tilly's floral perfume. She's on high alert, braced for any sudden movements, as though Tilly might, without warning, turn psycho and lunge at her, but Tilly is staring out of the window at the softly lit houses as they head away from their suburb toward the freeway.

"Gary wasn't interested in coming?" Claire asks, when Tilly doesn't volunteer anything more.

"Nah. He's a bit grumpy at the moment. Better to leave him at home."

Tilly continues to sit quietly, while Claire wonders if she dares bring up Silverlakes again. Instead, she asks, "How did you end up in Perth, Tilly?"

"Who wouldn't want to live here?" Tilly says, turning to Claire with a bright smile. "It's beautiful."

Tilly really is an expert at avoiding questions she doesn't want to answer. The conversation is so benign that Claire has the sudden urge to laugh.

Then Tilly adds softly, "And it's the perfect place to escape to when you need to start afresh, don't you think?"

Claire's hands squeeze the wheel, her heart in her mouth. Her mind goes to the gun in the bag behind her seat, wondering how quickly she can grab it if she needs to. But Tilly is smiling beatifically; not looking at all like a lunatic getting ready to lunge. At a loss for a decent response, Claire is so distracted that she realizes late that she's almost past the turn for the pub. She swings hard around the corner, the tires objecting with a screech, and Tilly lets out a gasp of alarm.

"Sorry," Claire says, trying to calm her breathing.

The venue lights sparkle in the distance. Beyond that, the ocean is inky purple in the almost dark. "Oh, I haven't been to this marina yet," Tilly says excitedly, leaning forward to peer out the window. "Although I wasn't expecting to make quite such an entrance," she adds with a laugh.

Claire's heart is still hammering from her erratic driving and Tilly's words. She pulls into the pub's parking lot and begins searching for a spot. When they stop, she sits back in her seat for a second, takes a big breath, and steadies herself.

"You okay?" Tilly is watching her curiously.

"Fine." Claire checks her phone. "Let's get inside; they're due to start in ten minutes."

They head across the parking lot toward the brightly lit entrance to the Oceanside. All of Tilly's casual remarks echo in Claire's head, but she doesn't know how to ask anything more. She can't win at this kind of verbal sparring. Tilly is too good at sidestepping and then delivering an uppercut of her own.

Inside the Oceanside, Claire stops in shock. She's never seen the place so full. The padded rows of seats down one side of the room are crammed with people, and every one of the numerous tables and chairs in the central space is taken. At one of the longer tables close to the stage Claire sees Saskia, and her heart sinks. She tries to look away before Saskia can spot her but isn't quick enough. Saskia stares at Claire, long and hard, then says something to her friends and shakes her head, and they look across before turning back to talk among themselves, occasionally glancing over and back again furtively, as though Claire is prey and they're deciding whether to pounce.

"Seems like all the seats are taken," Tilly says behind her. "I might just pop to the bathroom."

Claire finds a barstool and sits down next to the bar, ordering herself a wine. She debates ordering Tilly one too but decides to wait until she's back.

"Claire?"

To Claire's surprise, Elizabeth appears in front of her. She's dressed up to the nines, wearing a large kaftan with a sparkly belt and glittering gold sandals, and her hair is immaculately styled, but Claire immediately sees how anxious she appears. "Elizabeth, what are you doing here?" She glances around. "Is Jarrod with you?" She tries to swallow her unease at the thought. "I know you've sent a few messages, but I haven't had time to reply, and you really didn't need to come all the way down here . . ."

"No, I came alone. And I'm sorry to hijack your evening like this, but it's the only place I knew I'd find you, as I remembered you telling me about it—and it's just . . . it's just . . ." To Claire's alarm, Elizabeth's eyes brim with tears.

"Come with me," Claire says, leading Elizabeth out into the corridor close to the bathrooms. By the time they get there, Elizabeth is openly weeping.

"I don't want to keep you," she says, "tonight of all nights." She gestures to the pub floor. "I won't stay for long. It's just . . . Jarrod told me he found you at the arena and asked you to come back. I told him I'd come here and try to persuade you . . ." She wipes her face and takes a deep breath, looking Claire in the eye. "But please don't. He's been asking questions about you, and his determination to have you training me has nothing to do with me getting fit. He has his own agenda, and I think we both know what that is. He treats women like possessions, and you're a challenge now, because you've said no, and that's not what he's used to. He's done it before: he's created a nice little system of getting me personal trainers, seducing them with flowers and gifts, taking what he wants from them and then paying them off. I didn't even realize to begin with—I thought it was only me that made him act like such an arsehole."

Claire regards Elizabeth with dismay. So her suspicions are justified. "That's awful," she says. "I'm so sorry."

Elizabeth carefully wipes the rims of her eyes with her manicured fingertips, trying not to smudge her heavy eyeliner. "If I can't rescue myself, at least I can do something for you. I've wanted to leave him for a long time, but he's a vindictive man, and I've always felt it might just be safer to stay, you know. To let him think I'm in his pocket and live my life for the kids, enjoy the things I can, avoid him as much as possible, and pretend the belittling doesn't hurt. Even though it just . . . it feels like such a waste . . ." she pauses. "Of myself, of my life. Is that the most selfish thing to say when there are kids involved?" She stares pleadingly at Claire. "Do you understand what I mean?"

A thousand thoughts run through Claire's mind. She tries to think of what to say first and struggles. Eventually, just as Elizabeth is beginning to look despairing, she says, "I do understand. In some ways more than you know. Not because of Lenny," she says quickly, glancing toward the doorway into the main pub, aware of the sudden hush. "But I've known men like Jarrod. None of this is easy, in your situation," she says. "It's an impossible position he's put you in."

Elizabeth nods, as people begin to cheer. "I should go," she says. "He'll be wondering where I am, he likes to keep tabs on me. I'll say you wouldn't agree to coming back."

"You don't have to leave," Claire replies, catching her arm lightly, alarmed when she sees Elizabeth wince. She loosens her grip, and Elizabeth follows Claire's gaze down to her wrist—both of them registering the long sleeves in the hot room—and when she looks up again, a shared knowledge passes between the two women. "Can you stay?" Claire asks more gently. "The band's pretty good. At least have some time out for a little while?"

Elizabeth nods. "Okay. I'll stay for a bit. Thanks."

They head back into the bar just as the lights dim. Although the conversation is over, Claire is bursting with everything she could have said. *Should* have said. She can't leave this alone, after what Elizabeth just told her. Who knows how close Jarrod is to snapping; or what he'll do when Elizabeth is just an encumbrance he needs to get rid of.

At the very least, she could introduce Elizabeth to Devon—although Devon's age and knee issues mean he's less physically able than he used to be, and perhaps she should be encouraging him to take it easy. She has a sudden flash of herself stepping into Devon's shoes: helping abused women find the strength to carry on. Yes, she would like that. And she can start right now. She leans across and opens her mouth, intending to tell Elizabeth she wants to help. But then the band walks onto the stage, the audience begins to cheer. And her chance is gone.

Resigned to the delay, she turns her attention to Lenny and his bandmates, who are readying their instruments, doing the final adjustments to the microphones, smiling at the crowd.

Then Claire remembers Tilly, wondering where she's gone. At first she can't spot her but then she sees that Tilly is perched on a stool at the other end of the bar. Her gaze is fixed on the stage, a small smile playing at the corners of her lips, as though she has completely forgotten her surroundings, in anticipation of what's coming.

chapter twenty-five

LENNY

L enny had expected to be nervous as the band heads out on the stage, but what he's forgotten, until this moment, standing in front of the packed bar, is the sheer adrenaline rush of singing live.

Pete grabs one of the mics at the front of the stage. "Ladies and gentlemen, I present to you, live on stage and for one night only, our very own northern suburbs tribute band, the Liviiiing Legeeeends!"

The pub fills with roars and cheers, as Lenny picks up his guitar, and checks on the rest of the group, making sure Eddie, Dave, and Fletch are ready to go. They all wait, poised to begin, watching him for the signal.

"It's great to be here," he says and slaps his leg four times to a steady beat, which is the agreed cue. As they strike up the first chords of Van Morrison's "Brown Eyed Girl," the crowd goes wild as soon as they recognize the tune, and by the time Lenny croons the first words a few people are beginning to sing along. He throws himself at every note, eyes mostly shut, nothing else existing in his head except the rhythm and flow of music, the sweetness of hitting each word at the perfect cadence. The reserved, harried dad that Lenny has become over the last five years quickly disappears, replaced by Lenny the showman, whose mind and body desire nothing more than to live inside the songs. Beside him he's vaguely aware of Eddie and Dave in full flow too, their bodies shimmying and swaying with the chords of their guitars.

They'd chosen this song first because it was short and a classic, a crowd-pleaser that instantly lifted everyone's mood and showed them that they were in for a good night. As they finish, Lenny opens his eyes and really looks into the audience for the first time.

Saskia is at the front with a large group of friends, at least half a dozen wine bottles and double the amount of half-filled glasses strewn across their long table, as they wave their arms in the air, singing along. She catches his eye, her face flushed and her eyes sparkling, and he gives her a quick flash of a smile of recognition before he begins searching for Claire. Because in a rush of euphoria he realizes he's been thinking about this all wrong. If she'd sent the flowers, for the reason Dave had suggested, perhaps it shows their marriage still has a chance. He's confused about the deception but more than anything he's glad she's here to see him. He wants Claire to remember him like this, when their lives had seemed so simple, and she'd sung along as she served the customers, and he'd watched and fallen in love with her before they'd even spoken a word.

He can't see her, but the pause between songs is growing too long, so he leans into the microphone, and sings the first lines to "American Pie" into the silent room. As he does, a few people whistle and there's a smattering of cheers, and by the time he reaches the chorus and the beat speeds up, everyone has joined in with him again.

He keeps scanning the room as he sings, eventually getting to the bar that runs along the back. It's too far away to make out all of the faces, many of them cast in shadow as they sit in places the room's spotlights don't reach. But then he thinks he sees her, right in the corner, leaning against the counter alongside a woman he doesn't recognize.

As the song finishes, someone opens a nearby door, and light washes over her for a moment.

It's definitely Claire.

He grins in her direction, convinced her presence is a sign that everything will be okay. Whatever is going on at home, and whoever is needling them, they'll get through it together. His body feels lighter as he sings "Walk this Way," followed by "Livin' on a Prayer," "The Horses," and "The Voice."

Lots of people are on their feet by the time the first half of the performance comes to an end. Saskia and her friends are standing on their chairs, whooping and cheering. At the back, Claire has hardly moved, and he wants to rush across to her, but instead he reluctantly follows his band members into the private rehearsal room, where four foaming pints of beer wait for them on a small table.

"Amazing!" Fletcher says. "I'd totally forgotten what a rush this is."

Dave and Eddie are smiling too. "Yes, but we've got to stay on our game for the second set," Eddie says. "We've practiced those songs a lot less than the first lot."

"We'll be fine," Lenny assures them. "I just need to duck out for a second." He turns without waiting for a response.

"Where are you going?" Dave calls from behind him, but Lenny doesn't answer. He hurries down a corridor that leads to the parking lot and goes around the outside of the building so he can come inside again close to the spot where Claire is standing.

He walks up behind her. "Got a moment?" he whispers in her ear.

She jumps, and whips around so quickly, with such apprehension on her face, that he's taken by surprise. "Whoa there, steady," he says, catching her at the elbows as her arms move to wrap defensively around herself. "Sorry, I didn't mean to give you a shock."

"Ah, the lead singer," says a gruff voice close by. "What an honor."

Lenny looks up to see a middle-aged man wearing a sharp suit and a smirk. The man offers his hand. "Jarrod . . ."

All Lenny's euphoria vanishes. He knocks Jarrod's hand away. "I know who you are, mate. And you can stay away from my wife."

A woman close by with a shiny face full of heavy makeup, and her fingers adorned with gold rings, puts her hand on Jarrod's chest as he takes a step forward. "Jarrod, we should leave."

Jarrod steps toward Lenny anyway. "Be careful who you pick a fight with, *mate*," he says, letting the woman pull him away but continuing to glare at Lenny.

"I know you've been harassing Claire," Lenny insists, struggling for composure. "Whatever you're after, it stops now. Don't mess with us, or next time we're calling the police."

Jarrod looks astonished, glancing around at all of them,

then he laughs sardonically. "I haven't got a clue what you're talking about! I just offered your wife a job. So go ahead, sue me!" He turns to Elizabeth. "Come on, I think it's time to go."

Lenny is left standing beside Claire, staring at Jarrod and Elizabeth as they make a hasty retreat, Jarrod's fingers firmly gripping Elizabeth's arm. People jostle around them, ordering new rounds at the bar. As the drinkers recognize Lenny they call out congratulations and encouragement, so before he gets waylaid, Lenny grabs Claire's hand. "Come with me."

She follows him out into the parking lot, where it's drizzling with light rain.

"What did you think about Jarrod?" Claire asks.

Lenny shrugs. "No idea. He looked genuinely surprised when I called him out."

"I know." She sighs. "He's a creep, but let's rule him out of anything else for now. Anyway, how are you feeling? Are you happy with how it's going tonight?"

"Yeah, actually." Lenny grins. "It feels good. What do you think? Have we still got it?"

"I reckon you have," she says, smiling back at him. "Did the casino guy turn up? You should definitely be doing this more often."

"Yeah, he's in there somewhere." He studies Claire's expression, trying to decide how much to say. "Are you sure everything's okay for now?"

"Yes. Devon won't leave until I'm back, don't worry."

"Right. That's good." Lenny hesitates, then adds, "I know you sent those flowers, Claire."

She frowns. "What?"

He hesitates. She doesn't look annoyed at having been

caught out, he thinks, with the first twinges of alarm; she seems utterly confused.

"The flowers . . . Dave checked out the purchase for me, and he said you sent them. At least," he adds, doubt washing over him as she appears to be in shock, "it was your credit card that paid for them."

Claire digs her phone out of her pocket and begins pressing the screen. Lenny moves closer and sees she's checking her online banking.

They both see the transaction. "That's it," she says. "But I didn't send them. Someone must have my credit card number."

"Oh."

Claire quickly rummages through her bag and grabs her purse. She opens it and looks through. "My card—it's gone."

Lenny can feel himself reddening. "Shit. Sorry. Dave thought you were trying to make me jealous."

She looks surprised. "Really?" She seems to sense he needs more because her expression darkens. "Perhaps I am a bit jealous of Saskia," she says, "but I can assure you I don't play stupid games with bunches of flowers."

They stare at one another in confusion.

"Lenny!" Dave's voice breaks the impasse, and Lenny turns to see him leaning out of the doorway. "We need you back in here now."

Claire leans forward and squeezes his arm. "Go," she says. "I'll see you afterward."

"Lenny!" Dave calls again, his irritation clear.

His heart in his mouth, Lenny takes one last look at Claire, puts his hands on her cheeks to cup her face, and kisses her, as tenderly as he can, before he walks away.

chapter twenty-six

CLAIRE

A s Claire turns to go back into the pub, she's already pulling out her phone. She texts Devon, checking all is okay at home, and then scans her online banking again, checking for other unauthorized transactions. It's easy to do since she hardly uses her credit card, and she can't find anything else that stands out. She screenshots the phone number she'll need to call to cancel her card, trying to decide whether it can wait until the band has played their second set; then her mind moves back to Tilly. On the journey home, she needs to confront Tilly about Silverlakes and all those sidelong comments, and insist she gives more than her usual cryptic answers. Too much has happened now to leave it alone.

She turns around to head inside and finds Saskia staring at her from the top step into the pub's alcove entrance, her bottom lip trembling and her eyes glassy.

"How long have you been standing there?" Claire asks.

"Long enough to see him kiss you. So," Saskia says with a hurt gleam in her eye, "I guess it's clear where Lenny's loyalties lie."

Claire swallows hard. The open marriage was never going to work, was it? It had just been an attempt to put off confronting her own issues. And now someone else is going to get hurt.

"Saskia," she says, "no one meant for it to end up like this. I'm sorry . . ."

"Lenny and I have something special," Saskia interrupts, her chin jutting out defiantly. "But he's a good guy—and you have children together. So of course he's going to stick with you. I should have known. If you don't let him go, he'll never leave."

Claire's hackles begin to rise. "It's not like that," she says, even as another part of herself is warning her to stop talking and allow Saskia her say.

"Whatever," Saskia says dismissively, walking down the steps closer to Claire, "but when you start rejecting him again, he'll come running back to me. Back to my *bed*," she adds, "because it's clear there are things I can give him that you can't, you frigid cow."

Claire feels the air leave her body as clearly as if Saskia had marched across and punched her in the stomach. The rage rises too fast for her to stop it. She clenches her fists and steps forward until she is eye to eye with Saskia, who takes a few hurried steps back.

"If you think Lenny would enjoy hearing you talk like that, you don't know him at all," she says. "Please understand, you know *nothing* about me or my marriage, Saskia, and you know *nothing* about what I'm capable of doing to protect my family. Be very, very careful about what you say to me, because right now I am this close," she pinches her fingers directly in front of Saskia's nose, "to losing my temper, and you don't want to be around me when I do." She grabs Saskia's arm. "Tell me the truth, are you behind all the crap that's been happening?" she demands, working hard to restrain herself from giving the woman a shake.

They are too close to one another for Claire not to see a hint of some sort of recognition in Saskia's eyes. "You're sick," Claire bursts out. "You sent the texts, didn't you? And the flowers? You put the camera in the house?"

But Saskia's frown is rapidly turning to alarm and confusion. "I don't know what you're talking about."

Claire loosens her grip and Saskia pushes her away. "You're mad, and I have no idea what he sees in you," she says in disgust, turning and running up the stairs and into the pub.

Claire leans back against the wall, trying to summon up the energy to go back in, when Saskia reappears, sobbing, leaning into the arms of a woman dressed in a bright red pantsuit and glossy black heels, surrounded by her tribe of fussing, clucking women, their night obviously over in solidarity with their friend. Claire moves quickly into the portico of the kitchen entry, hoping they don't turn and spot her, but no one pays her any attention. The women are all focused on Saskia, hurrying her toward the parking lot.

Once they've gone, Claire heads back inside to search for Tilly. The barstool where she'd been sitting earlier has been taken by another woman with a low-cut dress, knee-high boots, and a mop of tight curls. Claire hurries over. "Excuse me, I'm trying to find my friend. She was sitting here earlier. She has cropped black hair and a nose stud. Have you seen her?"

"No, sorry," the woman shrugs.

Claire turns to see the band are making their way back on stage. As soon as Fletcher is behind the drums and the others have picked up their guitars, Lenny launches into Queen's "Don't Stop Me Now" and the audience cheers. Those who've been outside begin to come back in and suddenly the pub is packed again, and there's not much room to move. Claire slowly makes her way to the side of the room, ignoring the irritated glances and mutters from those she pushes past, trying to get a better vantage point from which to spot Tilly. As Lenny hits his stride, she scans the room, trying to check each face methodically.

She can't see Tilly anywhere.

She scans the room again. She's desperate to go as soon as the set is finished, but she doesn't want to leave her new neighbor stranded without a ride. Damn it, if Tilly really wanted a lift, she should have stuck closer.

Claire uses a gap between songs to slowly push her way through the crowd again so she's close to the exit. As she nears the door, Lenny launches into Coldplay's "Yellow," a song she's heard him sing a thousand times before. Emotion catches in her throat as she listens to the purity of his voice in each note. He knows she loves this song, and she hates the thought of him seeing her leave while he's singing it. She turns back for a moment, and sure enough, he's looking her way. She gives him the most reassuring smile she can, but then turns quickly, and heads out the door.

Outside, she grabs her phone, hoping Devon has replied. There's nothing from him, but there are four missed calls from a New Zealand number.

Mary-Rose.

Claire can hardly breathe as she sits heavily at the top of some shadowy stone steps that lead down to the harbor, and returns the call.

"Hello, love," Mary-Rose answers immediately. "Are you at home?"

"No, why?"

"I need to send you a photo. Can you look at it while you're on the line?"

"Yes—hang on—I'll put you on speaker."

Claire makes the switch and then sees Mary-Rose's text come up. "Do you recognize this woman?" she asks.

Claire's whole body begins to shake as she stares at the photo. A young woman with piercing blue eyes and a nose ring glowers back, her dark hair longer than it is now, but still unmistakably Tilly.

"Yes," she says. "That's Tilly, the woman who's moved in opposite us. Who is she?"

"I'm sorry, Claire—she's Ryan's wife."

"What? How is that possible?"

"She began visiting him in jail a few years ago and married him six months ago. I don't know what she wants, but you need to get yourself and your family someplace safe as soon as possible."

"You still don't know where Ryan is?"

"No—but I'm waiting for a call back right now from the warden. I'll insist on getting answers; I'll tell him lives might be at stake. I'll call you as soon as I've spoken to him."

Claire is only half listening as she glances back at the pub, knowing for certain that Tilly isn't there anymore. "I have to go," she yells, and sets off at a run, heading for her car. It only takes a few seconds to get there, but a couple of people are standing with their backs to her, staring at her vehicle.

As she gets closer, it takes a moment for her to realize what they're staring at. And then she sees it:

All her tires have been slashed.

chapter twenty-seven

LENNY

Everyone is on their feet by the time the band finish their encore with Pink's "Walk Me Home." As Lenny leaves the stage, he tries to absorb the applause, hoping he's fooled everyone into believing his energy levels were as high as an hour ago. But he'd seen Claire's exit in the middle of their favorite song, and that, coupled with Saskia's empty table, had caused all the adrenaline to rapidly drain from him, leaving him desperately mimicking an enthusiastic frontman. Now he's sweating heavily and close to exhaustion.

"Jeez, you're as soaked as I am," Fletcher says, wiping the sweat from his red face and grinning at Lenny as they get into the back room. "But the audience loved it, so kudos to you for holding them spellbound." He claps Lenny on the back. "Seriously, your singing was fucking awesome tonight, mate."

"Absolutely," comes a voice from behind them. Lenny turns to see Baz coming into the room, hand outstretched.

"You were on fire. Let's get a meeting together, eh, and talk about what you might bring to the casino venues."

The band members beam at one another, forming a semicircle with Baz to raise the fresh pints that the landlord has left for them, in a toast to their future gigs.

Behind them, the door opens, and a voice asks, "Is Lenny in here?"

Without thinking, Lenny turns and says, "That's me," still holding his glass in his hand. A small and wiry man with long, unkempt hair marches across in a fury and punches Lenny in the face.

In the split second before Lenny staggers backward, he sees Saskia peeping around the door with a satisfied smirk. As Lenny reels, he drops his pint, which smashes on the floor, spattering icy liquid across his shoes and the bottoms of his jeans.

Dave's quick reflexes manage to steady Lenny before he crashes to the ground. "What the hell are you doing—?" Dave roars.

"That's what you get for shagging my wife. Stay the fuck away from Saskia and my kids," the man shouts, backing out of the room as he points at Lenny.

Lenny gingerly touches his stinging cheek and presses his tongue against his throbbing lip, hoping it doesn't look too bad. Baz glances around at them all uncertainly. "I presume this isn't the usual aftershow event?"

Eddie glares furiously at Lenny before replying, "No, definitely not. I'm so sorry about that. Lenny's been having a few issues with his girlfriend."

"Oh?" Baz frowns. "I thought you were all married?"

"It's complicated," Eddie interrupts before Lenny can answer.

"Come on," Dave says to Lenny. "Let's go and get you some ice." He leads Lenny quickly into the corridor.

"Shit," Lenny says, "I've blown it for us, haven't I?"

Dave shrugs. "I'm sure Eddie will do some smooth talking. Don't panic."

Dave disappears and Lenny waits, hand against his throbbing lip, while bartenders skirt around him, balancing tall stacks of dirty glasses like circus performers. The comedown is happening fast now. Exhaustion is setting in.

"Lenny!"

Claire is hurrying down the corridor, and the horror on her face makes him take his hand away from his lip, barely registering the blood on his fingers.

"We have to go home, now, in your car. Someone's slashed my tires," she says, and then adds in a hoarse whisper, "And I just got this." She holds up her phone and he stares at the screen, hardly able to comprehend what he's seeing.

It's a picture of his mother, tearful and terrified, her hands bound in front of her, and a gag in her mouth.

He doesn't even think about collecting his belongings. Nor does he register the fact that his bandmates and Baz are all watching from the doorway and Dave has returned from the kitchen and is holding out a bag full of ice. He can't focus on anything but the terror on Claire's face, and the thought of his mum and kids at home; then he's sprinting with Claire toward his car.

chapter twenty-eight

CLAIRE

"**D**rive faster," Claire insists, as they just make it through a set of traffic lights on yellow.

"It's not going to help if we get pulled over," Lenny snaps. "I might be just over the limit too—I had a couple of pints back there. *Fuck*." He bangs his palms against the steering wheel. "We shouldn't have left them. How could we be so stupid?"

Claire is still staring at her phone screen and the short message that had accompanied the picture of Lydia. *Come home now. No police.*

"I thought we had it covered, with Devon there and Tilly coming with me," she says. "I've been trying to contact Devon, but he isn't replying."

"Why would someone do this? I don't understand."

Claire stalls for a moment, not wanting Lenny to panic while he's driving, but this isn't the time to hold back. "Mary-Rose called earlier and told me that Tilly is Ryan's wife."

178

"What the hell . . . ?" Lenny's voice cuts off as he brakes suddenly to avoid going through a red light.

"Apparently, she visited Ryan in prison. I don't know anything else yet."

"So what does she want? Is this about revenge? Is she insane? Is Ryan about to turn up too? Oh god, Claire, my mum . . . the kids . . . what is she going to do to them?" he asks, his voice high-pitched with distress.

"She'll probably do whatever she thinks will hurt me," Claire says dully. "Ryan will have gotten inside her head. It's been my nightmare for a long time—but I always imagined he would be the one who'd come for me, that he'd get out of jail somehow and track me down." She's overcome by a rush of horror. "Perhaps he's there too," she whispers, a catch in her voice, "waiting."

Lenny's eyes are manic as he watches the road, the car swerving sharply as he overtakes a slow-moving truck. "Can we do anything?" he asks. "Other than just walking into our house like sitting ducks and letting Tilly and her henchmen do whatever they like to us? Come to think of it, if she's married to Ryan, who the hell is Gary?"

Claire shakes her head in despair. "I don't know." She turns to Lenny. "Just be ready, won't you, to run as fast as you can with the kids as soon as you get the chance." As she speaks, she opens the bag on her lap, checking the gun, not wanting to take the safety off yet.

Beside her, she hears Lenny's sudden sharp intake of breath.

"Claire, why the hell do you have that?"

"To keep us safe."

He looks incredulous. "Do you even know how to use it?"

"Yes," she says, with such certainty that his eyes bulge as he glances between her, the gun, and the road.

"Who the hell are you?" he whispers.

Her jaw clenches, but she doesn't reply. Right now, she's not sure who she is either. Claire? Lucy? Or someone else? How far will she go to protect her family?

"Seriously, I don't think that's a good idea," Lenny says, nodding at the gun.

Before Claire can answer, her mobile rings. It's a number she doesn't know and as she presses answer, she puts it on speaker.

"You got my message then?" Tilly says, her voice light and breezy.

"Tilly, whatever you want," Claire answers carefully, "we can keep it between us. No one else needs to be involved. Please, let the others go."

"Not quite yet, Claire," Tilly laughs. "But no one needs to get hurt if you do what I say. Are you nearly home yet? Oh, hang on, I know exactly where you are. Turning off the freeway, yes?"

Claire and Lenny stare at one another in shock.

"We've had tracking devices on your cars for a week," Tilly says, "along with a little camera I left at your house. It's been pretty interesting watching where you've been and listening to your heart-to-hearts at home. You left out some important details last night, though, Claire. So, listen. When you get here, you need to park on your driveway. Lenny, you'll go inside your house, and Claire, you're to come across the road to me. You and I have a few things we need to discuss."

Before they can ask any more, she's ended the call.

180

"I need to call Mary-Rose," Claire says immediately, tapping on her phone and quickly putting it on speaker.

"Are you okay?" Mary-Rose asks as soon as she picks up, the worry clear in her voice. "What's happening?"

"We're driving home. I thought Tilly was at the pub with me, but she left, and I found my car tires slashed. I had a message on my phone telling us to come home and not to call the police—along with a picture of Lenny's mum tied up and gagged." Claire's voice breaks and she swallows hard. "You know this is what I've always feared, that Ryan would come after me. Can you tell us anything that might help?"

"I'm pulling up everything I can find," Mary-Rose says. "So far, I know that Matilda—Tilly—was the sister of a man in jail with Ryan. His name was Archer, but he committed suicide a few years ago. Tilly's listed on the visitors' register lots of times, first going to see Archer, then there's a gap before she begins seeing Ryan instead. The only other thing I can find out is that she was in and out of foster homes as a kid; she worked at a massage parlor for a long time—and not one of the respectable ones. So she hasn't said anything more about what she wants from you?"

"Not yet." Claire grimaces. "But I know it's revenge for Ryan, and I'll have to persuade her that this is between her and me. Because he'll already have given her his own twisted version of the story, and he's a first-class manipulator. They must have overpowered Devon somehow because he was keeping watch on the house while we were out."

"Keep the phone on," Mary-Rose tells her. "I can listen and record it and send for help."

"Okay," Claire says. "We'll call back when we're there."

181

Lenny cuts in. "In the meantime, call Oceanside police station, and ask them to get a message to Sergeant David Turner. Tell him that there's an emergency at Lenny's house. He'll take it seriously."

"I'll do it now," Mary-Rose says. "Wait a second, I've just got another email through from a contact at the prison."

She goes quiet for so long that Claire begins to panic. "Mary-Rose, are you still there? Talk to us!"

"Sorry, sorry," Mary-Rose says. "I was just scanning the details. It looks like there was an incident at Paremoremo. A fight between an inmate—Ryan—and a prison guard. The management hushed it up, so the guard didn't get in trouble. But it says here that Ryan has been in a coma for the last six months."

Relief rushes through Claire.

He's in a coma! He isn't here.

The respite lasts all of five seconds until Claire remembers Tilly's weird singsong tone; the comments designed to unnerve her; the strange happenings of the past week. In hindsight, she can see it all now: Tilly's faux friendliness had always been flecked with restrained fury.

Her breath catches. They might not have to deal with Ryan, but instead, they're about to face his traumatized, vengeful wife.

chapter twenty-nine

LENNY

As Lenny pulls into the drive, he vaguely realizes that he can't recall a second of the journey home. He feels like he's sleepwalking in someone else's life. Surely this can't really be happening to them.

He studies their darkened house, dreading what he's about to find inside.

"Lenny," Claire says, touching his leg. He flinches. "Whatever happens in there, be alert for opportunities but don't take unnecessary risks. Give me your phone." He hands it to her automatically, and she dials a number. "This is Mary-Rose," she says when it's connected. "Put it in your back pocket, with the speaker facing out."

He watches her push the gun into the back of her jeans' waistband. He wants to tell her to stay safe, but instead finds himself saying, "Don't die."

She flashes him a look he can't read. "I'll do my best. Come on, we have to go."

They get out of the car, and Lenny approaches their front door, trying the handle and finding it open. As he glances back, Claire gives him a quick nod.

He steps inside.

It's dark in the front hallway, but there's light coming from the living room. He walks slowly forward, light-headed and queasy from the fear of what he might see.

"Come on in, Lenny," calls a male voice. "We've been waiting for you."

Gary sits next to Lydia on the sofa, holding the tip of a long kitchen knife to her neck. Lydia's face is ashen, except for the places where her eye makeup has run down her cheeks in black patches. Her wrists are bound together with thick tape. Jake is cuddled into her, his head buried in her chest.

"Please," Lenny says, his voice breaking at the sight of his distressed son. "Now I'm here; let them go. I'll stay, and you can do whatever you want with me."

He's so intent on the scene in front of him that he almost trips over the body on the floor. As his foot connects, he looks down to see the man from the beach—Devon—unconscious, with his hands bound behind his back and a nasty gash on his forehead.

Lenny just stares. He's beginning to think he's hallucinating the whole evening, when Jake suddenly registers his presence and makes a dash for him, yelling, "Dad!"

"Hey," the man says, grabbing Jake and pulling him roughly backward onto the sofa. Lenny instinctively goes to yank Jake away, but the man is too quick with the knife, letting it settle against Lydia's throat again. "Control your kid," he snaps.

Lenny edges over to the sofa until he can perch on the arm, saying to Jake, "Hang tight, buddy."

"I hate you," Jake screams at Gary.

"Shhh," Lenny says, praying Jake will calm down, and not make the situation worse.

Jake seems to catch Lenny's thoughts. He falls quiet.

"Get down on the floor, Lenny, and put your hands behind your back," Gary says.

Lenny glances around at the others, weighing up whether he really has to do this, but everyone looks terrified. "Where's Emily?" he asks, as he slowly follows Gary's instruction.

Lydia lets out a moan.

"The lady took her," Jake says.

Lenny's chest burns as Gary quickly secures his wrists with cable ties.

"You mean Tilly took her?" he asks, staring at his mother for confirmation. Lydia nods.

"Right," Gary says, focusing on Jake. "Don't you move a muscle, or I'll have to tie you up as well." He kicks lightly at Devon. "And I might just kill your lizard as well."

Jake turns and buries his head back into Lydia's chest.

"And now," Gary says, putting his legs up to rest on Devon's back like he's a footstool, and settling back on the sofa. "We wait."

chapter thirty

CLAIRE

There's no answer when Claire knocks on Tilly's door, but when she tries the handle, the door opens into a dark entrance hall. There's a small empty room to her right, off the corridor leading farther into the open-plan house, where she can see there's some kind of dull light flickering in one corner.

"Welcome, Lucy," Tilly says from somewhere in front of her.

Claire walks toward the voice, every sinew snapping to attention, ready to react if something or someone jumps out without warning. But as she rounds the corner, her breath catches in horror.

Tilly sits on the floor in the corner of the empty room, Emily pulled against her in a one-armed hug, a kitchen knife sitting casually in the other hand. Emily looks like she's cried herself out, and stares in exhausted confusion at her mother. The sight of her little girl sitting there in her *Paw Patrol* pajamas almost undoes Claire. But the tiger inside her stirs too, beginning to prowl, waiting for its chance.

"I think she's catatonic," Tilly says lightly, peering around at Emily. "But it must be pretty stressful to find out your mum's a murderer." Her eyes narrow. "You're shaking, Claire. It's hard, isn't it, to see someone you love in distress?" Her voice deepens as she snaps, "Now, spin around slowly." She feigns shock as Claire does so. "Oh, I think you have something stuck in the back of your jeans. Throw that here, won't you."

Claire bends down and sends the Beretta scooting along the floor, relieved that the safety is still on, giving her at least a chance to react if Tilly makes a move to use it.

"Anything else you got there? Knives? Flamethrowers?" Tilly laughs, pulling the gun closer to her so that it rests by her side. "Your mum is very resourceful," she says in a loud whisper into Emily's ear.

Claire holds her hands aloft. "No, there's nothing else. And you don't need to keep Emily here. I'll cooperate and do whatever you want."

"Thanks, but no, I think we'll work well together like this. We won't be long."

"It was all you, then?" Claire asks. "The texts, the flowers, as well as the camera . . ."

Tilly sniggers. "Of course. Who else would it be? Or have you made lots of enemies here too, Claire? I have to say, you made it so easy to mess with you: you leave your keys on a hook by the door, your bag on the side table. I had access to your house and money in seconds. You should really be more careful."

"And did you take the lizard too?"

"Oh yeah, Bob's lucky to be alive," Tilly laughs. "I wanted to kill the little pest and put it back just to freak you out, but Gary said it was too much too soon and I needed to bide my time. So here we are at last," she adds with a scowl. "I've been waiting for this moment for so long."

"What do you want from me?"

"You see that table and chairs over there?"

Claire looks toward where Tilly is pointing. On a small melamine table, she sees a phone set up on a small portable tripod. "You need to sit on the chair opposite the camera," she says, gesturing to it, "and read what's on the sheet."

Claire goes across, sits down, and picks up the typed piece of paper. The speech that has been written for her is short and simple.

My name is Lucy Rutherford. Eleven years ago, I faked my own death in Tetherton, New Zealand, leaving Ryan Doherty to take the blame for the death of my boyfriend Todd. However, the truth is, I told Ryan to kill Todd. I am the one responsible for his death. And I cannot live with myself anymore.

Claire stops reading and looks up. She wants to tell Tilly that surely this won't make any difference. There was a trial. Ryan killed Todd, and he deserved his sentence—which was nothing compared to the trauma Todd's family and friends would endure forever. But she can't say any of that while Tilly's arm is wrapped tightly around Emily. So she just says, "Okay. But can you tell me why? What do you hope to get out of all this?"

"A happy ending, of course," Tilly says immediately.

"Tilly, I know about Ryan," Claire asks cautiously.

"Shut up. Don't you even talk about him, don't you *dare* say his name!" Tilly shouts, brandishing the knife toward Claire so that Emily squeals and Claire immediately holds her hands aloft. "He's all I've got now," she says. "Since Archer died."

"Tell me about Archer," Claire asks, desperate to keep Tilly talking while she figures out how to get Emily out of her grasp.

"My brother? Our parents were druggies—they didn't give a shit about us. Archer had to steal everything we needed. He kept us alive, and he never wanted to hurt anyone, we just needed the money. But Archer got set up after a petrol station robbery went wrong and a man got run over—he took the blame when his mates ran off." There's a rising tremor in her voice. "I visited him all the time, trying to keep his spirits up, but they broke him in the end: the other prisoners, the whole fucking system. Ryan was his best friend inside. Ryan believed Archer, because he knew what it was like to be in there when you shouldn't be. After Archer OD'd, and I had no one left, I went to visit Ryan and thank him for being Archer's friend. As soon as we began talking, I knew he was the one." Tilly gazes into the distance, momentarily lost in the past. "We got married pretty quickly, and it was the best day of my life. But just like my brother, he'd been left to rot, and we'd never get the chance to have a proper life together. And that," she says, her tone hardening as she waves the knife at Claire, "was because of you."

Claire thinks of objecting, of telling Tilly how much she's got wrong, but she knows Tilly wants to talk, not listen, and it won't be a good idea to anger her. So she grips the sides of her seat hard as Tilly continues, her words coming fast in high-pitched accusation, "*You* told him to kill your boyfriend, and he did it because you'd bewitched him and he loved you. He knew it was wrong, but you had a hold over him and he couldn't shake it—he talked about you like you were a witch or something. Are you a witch, Claire?" Tilly adds with a cackle that makes Emily's lip tremble. Claire shudders. Trauma is one thing, but insanity is another; she can only hope to talk Tilly down if she hasn't already jumped off the edge of reason. She fixes her eyes on her daughter, hoping she can transmit some small reassurance to her that this is going to be okay.

Tilly is still talking. "Ryan's always said that our only hope of being together and him getting free was to find you and get you to finally admit what you'd done. He knew you hadn't killed yourself; he's not stupid."

"So how did you track me down?"

Tilly bares her teeth as she smiles. "I went to see your sister."

Claire freezes. Quickly, she reminds herself that Mary-Rose has already said that Candace is okay.

"My sister doesn't even know I'm here."

"Well, she might do if she bothered to search for you. I pretended I was a nurse and got chatting with her. She was super friendly; it didn't take long before she invited me to lunch. She didn't admit to your existence, though—said she only had a brother when I asked." Claire tries not to react, but Tilly must sense she's struck a nerve. "Yeah, hurts to think you've been forgotten, doesn't it? Even if you did bring it on yourself." Tilly snorts. "Anyway, I didn't have to look far to find that photo of you at your wedding, she had it up on her fridge."

The pang in Claire's chest is painful. Candace had put that

photo somewhere she could see it every day. That wasn't the choice of a sister who wanted to forget—but rather one determined to remember. Her family haven't forgotten her.

Her relief is followed by a fresh wave of determination as she glances at Emily. She's sick of causing the people she loves so much pain.

"I took that photo and showed it to Ryan," Tilly continues. "He was convinced we could find out where you were, so I rang around to a lot of wedding chapels in Vegas, let me tell you. But we got there in the end. Impersonating a private detective has its uses when it comes to getting information. But before I could even visit Ryan to say I'd found you, he got bashed by some psycho. Hit his head on a concrete floor, and he's been in a coma ever since."

Claire clutches the edge of the table, her head swimming as Tilly confirms Mary-Rose's words. She wants to cry and rage with relief and bitterness. Ryan hasn't been able to pursue his vendetta for months, and yet he's still found a way to destroy her. She breathes heavily, drawing together all the strength she has, knowing she can't let Tilly see any emotion. "I'm sorry," she says.

Tilly snorts. "No, you're not. I'm sure you'd bring out the champagne if I told you he was dead. But he isn't yet. And I realized . . ." Tilly hesitates, and Claire watches her struggling to maintain her composure. The anger vanishes for a moment, leaving Tilly looking lost and bereft. " . . . that if I found you, and got you to confess, it might be enough to wake him up. If he knows there's still a chance of us having a life together—and making our own family," she says, giving Emily a squeeze, "then he might feel there's more to live for."

The room falls silent. But then Tilly's voice hardens as she adds, "The last time I saw him, I promised I'd do whatever it took to find you and get justice. So here we are. And now you know what you need to do."

chapter thirty-one

No one has said anything for a long while; the only sound in the room is the steady tick of the clock on the wall.

"What's in this for you?" Lenny asks Gary. He's been plucking up the nerve to speak while lying facedown on the floor, figuring that if he can ask questions, he might discover something he can use to get under Gary's skin.

Gary doesn't speak for a moment, and Lenny thinks perhaps he isn't going to answer, but then he says, "I'm keeping a promise."

"To Tilly?"

"I knew her brother. He helped me out a lot. I told him I'd take care of her."

"Would he want her doing this?" Lenny asks. "If it means she might end up in jail?"

Gary laughs. "She's not going to end up in jail."

He sounds so sure that Lenny's mouth goes dry. He focuses on Devon, lying beside him on the cold floor. Blood has run from the cut on Devon's forehead into his left eye and down his cheek. His skin is gray, and he's so still that Lenny would fear the man had already stopped breathing if not for the slow rise and fall of his chest.

He has to try something. "I can hear sirens," he says.

"Bullshit," Gary snaps.

Lenny shifts slightly, his belt cutting into his hip bones and his skin cold against the tiled floor. "Maybe the police are outside," he persists. There's a silent pause as all of them concentrate on the noises in the distance. They stay like that for a minute, and then Gary sighs and says to Jake, "Come here, let's check who's outside." And they disappear to the front of the house.

To Lenny's surprise, his mother moves the instant they're gone, crouching down beside him, her bound hands awkwardly pulling at Devon's jacket. She pauses for a moment to pull at the gag against her mouth. "He reached for something," she rasps. "Before he got knocked out. Here." Her fingers clutch at a small flick-knife, but Gary's voice is getting louder as he returns down the hall, and in a panic, she throws it at Lenny, who shuffles fast to lie on top of it while his mother sits back on the sofa.

Gary pushes Jake toward the sofa ahead of him and then sits down with a thump, picking up his phone and holding it to his ear. "You done yet? Things are getting jumpy here." There's a pause while he listens, before he says, "Okay, okay."

Lenny is wriggling slowly, working his body until his fingers reach the knife. Once he has a tentative grasp, he pries the small blade open and begins to fiddle with it, trying to position it between his fingers so he can get a sawing motion going against the cable tie.

Gary ends the call and begins to rummage in a small black bag. He brings out a can of petrol and shakes it over the sofa, spreading a trail of it along the walls to the curtains. Lenny has to twist to see what Gary's doing, but he can see his mother sit up as she registers the liquid in her lap, starting to panic.

Lenny works quickly with the knife, trying to ignore the sharp pains where his fingers accidentally meet the blade. The task is excruciating, and he loses his grip a number of times before finally beginning to make an impression on the plastic tie. His skin is slick with what he fears is blood, but he has the right tension now and continues to saw awkwardly against the binding.

"Well, it's been a pleasure, but it's almost time for me to go," Gary says, standing up and pulling a lighter from his pocket, flicking it on and off idly while glancing at his phone.

One minute there's stillness, and then suddenly Lenny rears up, pulling his arms free. He lets out an almighty growl and shoves Gary backward, the knife making contact with Gary's right palm, and the advantage of surprise sending the bigger man flying.

Gary roars with rage, pushing himself up without seeming to register his bleeding hand. Jake comes full pelt toward him, intending to defend his dad, but Lenny reaches out to scoop up his little boy, whips around, and almost throws Jake toward the front door. "Run and hide," he hisses. "Now!" he adds with such ferocity that Jake takes one look at his face and races away.

chapter thirty-two

CLAIRE

Claire presses record and reads the script to the camera.

"Do it again," Tilly snaps straightaway. "And put some effort in, so it sounds like you mean it."

"Mummy," Emily whispers, "I need the toilet."

The problem seems to have brought Emily out of her stupor, and she looks pleadingly at Claire.

"I just have to do this one more time," Claire says reassuringly, "then we can get you out of here." She reads the script as quickly and convincingly as she can, putting gravitas behind each word. She doesn't know if there will be repercussions if this finds its way online or to the authorities, but she doesn't care right now, while all of their fates are in her hands.

"Now throw the phone here," Tilly says when Claire has finished, her grip tightening around Emily.

In response, Claire deliberately pushes the phone along the floor so it only skids halfway toward Tilly.

"Don't play games!" Tilly snaps. "I know what you're doing. Don't move a muscle, I'll get it."

Tilly shuffles forward with Emily firmly in her grip, and grabs the phone, but, just as Claire had hoped, she doesn't go back to the corner. The distance between them has halved.

"I've done what you asked," Claire says. "Now at least let Emily go. You don't need her anymore."

Tilly ignores her. "First you need to see this," she says, her fingers moving swiftly over the phone screen as she first checks Claire's recording and then keeps scrolling. Tilly's movements are jerky, and Claire realizes they are both trembling. After a moment Tilly throws the phone back to Claire, and Claire picks it up and then almost drops it in horror. Ryan's face fills the screen, except for the little triangle that shows it's a video, which is displayed across his mouth.

"Watch it," Tilly insists. "He made this a long time ago because he knew I'd find you sooner or later. It's rushed because I had to do one of the guards a favor so he'd look away for a couple of minutes—but you'll get the message."

Claire stares at her wildly, but when Tilly tightens her grip on Emily and the child moans, she reluctantly presses play.

"Hello, Lucy," Ryan says in a singsong voice. "I knew Tilly would find you. Did you really think you could just run away and leave me here to rot?" He leans right into the camera so his face fills the screen. "Bitch," he adds, with a wink, "your time is up."

Claire can barely stop her body from shaking. As soon as she registers his final words, her panicked gaze swings back to Tilly.

"Do you really think," Tilly says, her voice unsteady and her fingers toying with the knife, glancing between it and the gun and Claire, "that you get to keep playing happy families, when Ryan and I will never have that chance? Do you think I would just leave and let you go? Didn't you hear what you said on that video? *I cannot live with myself anymore.*"

Claire stills, as her senses explode: the dark room is a pulsing, throbbing time bomb.

"And of course, a selfish person like you would take your whole family with you. They'll call it a murder/suicide when they find your charred bodies in your house." Tilly's grin is maniacal. "Gary's prepping your house right now, so it'll go up in seconds when you're all dead."

"But why?" Claire pleads, playing for every snatch of time. "I understand me, but Tilly, do you really want to kill an innocent man and his kids? And their grandmother too—she's done nothing in all this. She thought you were great, and she doesn't even like me," Claire lies, desperate for anything that might jolt Tilly out of this terrible plan.

And she can see it hits a nerve. A muscle in Tilly's jaw twitches. But then she says, "Ryan told me if I ever found you, I had to make you understand what it's like to have everything you love taken from you. So now," she says, lifting the gun to Emily's temple, "it's time for you to find out."

Claire lunges forward, knowing she has only a second to react before Tilly realizes the safety is still on. She knocks them all off balance, and Claire yanks a screaming Emily behind her as she wrestles Tilly for the gun. But Claire's grip is far stronger than Tilly's, and Devon had taught her how to twist a wrist to release a weapon. As the gun comes into her hands, she releases the safety.

Tilly stops as though realizing she is in trouble. Claire edges back, pointing the gun at Tilly, who suddenly leaps forward, slashing the air with her knife, catching Claire's forearm so that she almost drops the weapon, leaving a line of blood.

As Tilly lets out a bark of delight, Claire understands that there will be no reasoning, no second chances for everyone in this room. Emily is huddled behind Claire's legs. And Claire is her child's last line of defense.

As Tilly lunges once more with the knife, Claire raises the gun.

chapter thirty-three

LENNY

Gary picks up a brass lamp and is about to bring it down on Lenny, but Lenny body-charges him, despite being only half the size of the man, and does enough to knock him off balance. Gary rights himself and takes a swing at Lenny with the lamp, connecting with his jaw with a crunch. Lenny falls onto the sofa, losing his grip on the flick-knife, turning just in time to see Gary lunging with his own blade. Lenny swerves at the last moment so that Gary misses him, and Lydia screams.

Lenny jumps to his feet, and the two men circle each other. Gary makes a few lunges at Lenny, who manages to avoid him, but on the last attempt, Lenny stumbles, knocking into the TV, which wobbles and then crashes backward against the wall. Gary lets out a bark of triumph and rushes at Lenny, who only has a second to right himself. Time slows as Lenny waits to feel the knife in his stomach, but before Gary reaches him, he doubles over, roaring.

As Gary crumples to the ground, Lenny sees that his mother is half-lying across Devon, and the flick-knife that Lenny had dropped on the couch is embedded in the flesh at the back of Gary's thigh. Blood begins to pulse from it as Gary huddles against the sofa, and Lenny realizes his mother is wailing, having thrown all her energy into this last desperate effort to save her son. Gary tries to snatch up the lighter, but Lenny is there first, hurling it into the far corner. Then he pulls his mother up, releases the gag from her mouth, and unties her. "Go find Jake," he hisses urgently, and she runs toward the front door.

Lenny upturns the black bag, noticing that Devon is beginning to stir. Cable ties scatter, and Lenny grabs one and goes for Gary's feet. Gary kicks out over and over until Lenny presses his thumb into the bleeding wound in Gary's thigh. Gary pauses and lets out a roar, but it's long enough for Lenny to get his feet tied together. Lenny gets off him and watches Gary frantically pull at the plastic binding.

"I think you need this," Lenny says, waving the switchblade at Gary from a distance. Gary lunges furiously and falls forward onto his face. Lenny seizes his chance and sits on Gary's shoulders, grabbing Gary's wrists and pulling them together. Devon is groggy now but on his knees. He throws his weight across Gary's upper back, allowing Lenny to secure another tie. Once he's done, Lenny helps Devon up and away from Gary, who's still twisting and writhing in a growing pool of blood.

The men gather their breath, chests heaving, as Gary lets out a series of guttural roars. Lenny quickly releases Devon's bindings, then grabs Devon's arm and just says, "Claire."

Both men rush to the front door. Lenny races toward the

redbrick house with Devon at his heels. He is about to charge inside when Devon catches his arm. "Careful," he says, "we may only get one chance."

They both creep toward the front door, just in time to hear Claire scream, "No!"

There's a beat of silence. And then a gunshot so loud that Lenny instinctively crouches with his hands over his head. A second later Lenny is kicking at the door, which swings open without resistance. He charges inside, blood pulsing through his ears, and collides with Claire, clutching Emily tightly to her, both of them smeared with blood. Claire stares at Lenny, her eyes wild. "Take her," she says, pushing Emily into his arms and turning back into the house.

"Mummy!" Emily screams as Lenny hurries her away. There are sirens now, getting closer every second, as Lydia and Jake huddle together in the front lawn. Neighbors are opening their doors, peering out in shock as they see the commotion.

Lenny hurries to Lydia and sets Emily down gently beside her. Emily buries herself in her grandmother's embrace, as Lenny puts an arm around his mother. "Are you okay?"

At Lydia's nod, as the first police car turns into the street, he jogs back across the road, and into the house opposite. He goes inside, following the sound of low murmurs, and sees Devon and Claire leaning over the prone form of Tilly. Claire is murmuring something, and Lenny watches from a distance. "Is she alive?" But even as he asks, he can see from their body language that there's no urgency to the situation.

Claire gets up slowly and comes toward him, her gaze steady, leading him back outside. She leans her head against his chest, her voice muffled as she whispers, "I am so, so sorry."

The pain of everything Lenny's seen and heard in the last few days runs through him. He knows already that there is a long journey ahead of them. He wants to shake her. Shout, rage, and cry all at once.

But right now she's leaning on him, trembling. And so he puts his arms around her, grateful he still has the chance to hold her hand.

chapter thirty-four

CLAIRE

I t's daybreak by the time they finish helping the police. They had asked Claire to recount over and over the moment she had lifted the gun and pulled the trigger. Where she'd been standing; what had been happening. They'd been sympathetic; she was, after all, a mother intent on saving her child's life. That was heroic and brave, one of them had said, as Claire had replayed the same scene over and over in her head: seeing Tilly crumple to the floor, an arc of blood spraying across the wall. Emily's eyes had been squeezed shut as Claire wrapped her arms around her daughter's trembling little body, covering it with her own.

At Lydia's house, a police officer lets them in. Lydia has gone ahead with the children, and the three of them are now cleaned up and fast asleep together on Lydia's double bed. The first thing Claire is going to do, she decides, is to give them the biggest, tightest hug she can when they all wake up. And that includes Lydia.

Lenny hadn't said much in the car, and nor had she. Claire has no idea how they will begin to get through this. Because it turned out the secrets she'd worked so hard to keep hadn't protected any of them, in the end.

"I feel like I should be going straight to bed," Lenny says, once the policewoman has checked they have what they need and left, "but I'm not tired at all. It'll take a lot to wind down from the amount of adrenaline that's gone through me over the last forty-eight hours." He walks over to the kitchen and begins to fill the kettle. "Do you want a drink?"

"Yes, okay," Claire says, her arms wrapped around herself as she looks around Lydia's house, which is full of floral decor and homemade embroidery. It's good to be somewhere new. And safe. She's certain they won't ever go back to their old house again. And yet she still can't stop her entire body from shaking.

Lenny takes a long look at her, then collects some glasses and pours her a whiskey instead.

"It might take me a while to believe we're safe," she says as she takes it from him with both hands.

"Yeah, I think it's going to take us all some time," Lenny agrees. He heads over to open Lydia's patio doors, sitting on the step and staring out into her small but beautifully maintained backyard, watching a few bees buzzing around the lavender bushes.

Claire wants to sit next to him. "And the kids are probably going to need professional help."

"At least there are no more secrets," Lenny says. "Perhaps we can finally move forward if it's all out in the open."

Claire nods, sipping her whiskey, staring at the tips of

205

the swaying trees beyond the garden. From her stillness, she thinks, Lenny would never guess the war raging inside her. But perhaps he knows her better than she thinks, because he suddenly says, "I need to ask you about one thing."

She grips the drink tightly, the glass warm and smooth in her hands. "What?"

"You and Devon. When I came into the house, after Tilly was shot, you were in a huddle, talking quickly to one another. What was that about?"

She doesn't answer immediately. She thinks of carrying this small thing alone for the rest of her life—because what she says next might forever alter whether Lenny sees her as his wife and a mother, or as a monster.

But she'd tried that before: living with a wound that festered and grew if it wasn't allowed air to heal. So she says, "Devon made sure I was going to deny all knowledge of the gun and tell the police it was Tilly's. And . . . and he asked me if I'd shot to wound or kill—because he'd trained me to do both."

She turns to look Lenny squarely in the eye, as he says steadily, "And what did you say?"

"I told him I aimed for her heart. And . . . he said he would have done the same." She stares at her hands for a moment, before turning back to Lenny. "Because he knows how hard it is to live with yourself after killing someone, even if you didn't think there was a choice," she adds. "And he doesn't want me to struggle with that alone."

Even now, she is already thinking of how young Tilly was, how vulnerable; her life a long series of traumas that she'd had no control over. If there'd been time, perhaps she could have reasoned with her? Told her that Ryan had always left a trail of shattered lives behind him, and Tilly was the latest. That he was a master manipulator, and she would never have had a family with him, because even if he woke up from his coma—which was a slim to zero chance according to Mary-Rose, who'd now managed to speak to the prison warden—he would be in jail forever after what he did. If only she could have talked Tilly down somehow and given her a second chance.

"There's something else I want you to know," she says suddenly. "About what happened to Todd."

She sees Lenny tense. His eyes don't leave hers. "Okay."

"That night," she says, speaking quickly before the truth can lock itself inside her again, "when Ryan took me and Todd hostage while he was high on meth, he pulled a knife on us and insisted we get in his car. Then he drove us an hour south to his small rented house in Silverlakes, tied Todd up, and sliced through both his Achilles tendons. He taunted him for a while about how he'd never run again, as Todd went in and out of consciousness because of the pain and blood loss. And then he asked me to choose who I wanted to be with. He counted down from ten—and when he reached two, I said I wanted him. I thought if I said Todd, Ryan would kill him—or me. Or both of us. So I said Ryan in the hope he would spare us. But he finished counting down to zero, and then he told Todd I'd made my choice, and killed him in front of me."

Lenny studies her without moving, and she doesn't flinch or look away. After a while she can't bear the silence any longer.

"It has always felt like I was the one who did it," she confesses, dropping her gaze, a creeping numbness stealing over her as she talks. "And since then, I've never been sure who

I am anymore. Tonight I looked at Tilly's body and I felt no remorse, only relief. So, the question is, what have I become?"

As she speaks, she senses the dark thoughts licking at her, drawing her in, until Lenny puts a hand on hers, and gently squeezes her fingers. "I can understand that, after everything that's happened to you. But you know, don't you, that Ryan gave you an impossible choice? And he would have killed Todd whatever you said."

She nods, wishing she could feel anything beyond this cold, disconnected blur.

"I'm sorry I don't have all the answers, and I can't fix this for you," Lenny says. "But," he adds softly, "I can tell you one thing. While you figure everything out, and while you heal, I know exactly where you belong."

His words break through. Claire looks up, taking in Lenny's kind, open face, and leans her head on his shoulder. At last, something gives way inside her. Tears roll silently down her cheeks, and neither she nor Lenny tries to wipe them away. Finally, in the recesses of Claire's mind, the beast she has lived with for so long stops prowling and slips away into the shadows. Leaving Claire and Lenny sitting alone, together, watching the sky lighten.

acknowledgments

This story was a fun one to write, and a lovely interlude to the busyness and stresses of life in the crazy COVID times of 2021. I wrote some of it in a small studio down near Dunsborough on the south coast of WA, and for that I want to acknowledge the generosity of Stuart Chapman, who made the trip possible. Thanks to Tara Wynne for always having my back and ensuring my stories get out into the world. Thanks to Karen Yates and Bill Massey for their work, enthusiasm, and patience, all of which made the book better. Thanks to the team at Blackstone for championing my novels and for your ongoing support, particularly Anne Fonteneau, Hannah Ohlmann, and Ciera Cox. Huge gratitude to my mum Marian and my stepdad Ray for always being there. And all my love and heartfelt thanks to Matt, Hannah, and Isabelle, for making my world go round and being the best support crew I could wish for.

Pippa, you were helping me work by caring for Isabelle

when I wrote this, as well as supporting my writing in all sorts of ways, and now it's crazy you're not here to see it published. I write this thank you as if you're still with us, because I have definitely felt your loving presence since you've been gone. Our lives only touched quite briefly in the bigger scheme of things, but you changed me forever. I'll never forget you, or your courage, or the way that, in the end, you embodied all the things in life that truly matter. Your girls are amazing, and will continue to be, because of you.